Tab

Can't Take Back Yesterday
By: KB Manz
Bookbaby

Publishers since 2011

Prologue:

He sat in the near darkness of the house, waiting for her to return. Both of the parents were creatures of habit, which made the waiting even easier, as he made sure that the daughter of the house had plans that kept her away. She wasn't the one he was seeking, not tonight.

As he sat there, on the floor beside the curving steps that led to the second story, he took time to think.

This wasn't going to be a crime of passion. Nope, he had thought it all out, had made sure that the gun was clean and fully armed, and that the box of spare bullets sat on the floor next to the left side of his worn blue jeans.

When the door opened, he almost missed it, almost.

Isn't that how most of these stories start? The "killer" sitting in the darkened house, waiting for the "victim" to return, often times "saving" one so called innocent?

Well, that's not how my story goes. I'm not some cold blooded murderer and I didn't think any of this out, not a single part of it. I mean, yeah, I can plan like the next guy, but never in a million years do I think I would have had the nerve to plot out, let alone go through with a two person killing spree.

If you're interested to learn more, read on because like most people, I have a story to tell. It may not be a long story and no, I'm not going to go back through my childhood either, since it wasn't that exciting a time for me. Do you really want to hear about how I had a great time growing up? Or do you think that there's something evil lurking in my past that turned me into a cold blooded killer? As I said before, I have a story to tell, so let me get to it.

Two months earlier...

I didn't intend to kill my parents, well at least not at first. I just wanted answers and the truth, for once. You want to know the funny thing about all of this truth seeking? Until my world completely changed, I was fairly convinced that I lived in a house where honesty was valued and used on a daily basis. That's how my sister and I were raised, and it was part of why I didn't really get into a lot of trouble growing up. It just wasn't worth it when you had two parents who would rather spend time "discussing" what you did wrong and how you could improve. We didn't really get punished for things we did wrong, we just got discussions.

Anyway, back to why I wanted the truth. They always say that people hear the worst things when they eavesdrop, which is what happened alright.

I was home in my room listening to my iPod when I needed to charge it. Since I had left the cord downstairs in my jacket, I went down to get it. I figured that I could do some of my homework while I waited. It was something I did almost every day, get stuff out of my coat, head back to my room.

Did my parents ever argue? Yeah, who didn't have parents that argued? Usually it was about us and well, I never really listened much to it and things would blow over. No big deal but this time?

I don't know why I thought I needed to lurk and hear what was being said. Maybe because they were fighting and not just arguing and well, it was different so yeah, I thought I'd listen for a few minutes, no big deal, and then go back upstairs.

They say that if you're in the right place at the right time, you learn things that you wouldn't learn any other way. Guess that was the way with this fight. I was in the exact right spot at the exact right time and I heard an earful.

I heard so much that I barely made it to my room before I felt my legs give out. How could I not have known any of this? But I left at the exact wrong time too. Maybe if I had stayed and heard all of the fight, I would have learned the entire secret and then none of this would have had to happen.

I could have confronted them both. It was just us in the house, and maybe they could have explained things so that I would understand. The truth it seemed was only expected from their kids, and not from them, and I needed to learn the truth. I deserved that much even if hearing it spoken aloud and directly to me would make it all too real. Still, I deserved to know, didn't I?

Did my parents really think that my sister Devon and I would never figure this stuff out? Yeah, so both of our parents carefully guarded the information, keeping it from us for all these years. Here's the thing with keeping a secret though:

> *People always find out and when they find out on their own? It's a big, big deal. As with all secrets, they almost never stay that way for long since only one person can actually keep a secret.*

That's especially true with the internet and Instagram, Facebook and Twitter. I mean, you can break up with your girl at the movies and before you ever get back to your car, everyone's texting you, asking if you're Ok or offering to fix you up with someone new, better, hotter.

So, yeah, a secret doesn't have much of a chance of staying that way. There's another proven way to keep it though. You don't know me so it's not going to be easy to trust me on this. But there **is** another way.

My story will show you just what that is but I'm not going to come out and tell you here so don't even bother to ask.

Chapter One

I just turned eighteen the day it all went down. Eighteen years of age and officially an adult, at least in the state of Pennsylvania and pretty much everywhere else in the country.

I didn't feel any different, as I stood in front of my mirror shaving. Yeah, I do have to shave, just not every day. I didn't look any different. That was still me standing there with the brown hair that has a mind of its own, even if I do cop to stealing some of my mom's gel to keep it in place when I have a date. I also have green eyes, and tanned skin.

I worked as a lifeguard at the local beach all summer to make some extra spending money. I was determined not to be one of those kids that write home asking for money all the time. I mean, come on, they are paying for everything else. It's up to me to make some of my own for my personal stuff.

Most of the time, I have kinda pale skin, which I got from my mom, but my sister has it too. It's just how that worked out. According to my ex-girlfriend, I have soft, full lips made for kissing. I also have a real intense stare, when I focus on the person in front of me. Yeah, I know how that sounds, but well she's a girl and my ex so what do you expect?

I'm not all that tall either, just barely six feet, and because I have to be in shape for the job, I have some decent muscle tone. I can and do run for hours on the beach every morning and sometimes at night too. I'm not that bad looking, but girls don't swoon around me.

They do for my best friend, Jake. Jake is the high school football jock, with the broad shoulders and blonde hair. He's 6'5", weighs 220 and has blue eyes. Swoon worthy my sister would call him, since she's had a crush on him ever since she was ten years old. It's lucky for all of us that Jake only sees her as a little sister. He doesn't even flirt, or talk to Devon when he comes over, and you'd think she'd get over it already.

My dad is 6'3", weighs 227, and has the same brown hair that I have without that stare thing. Dad's eyes are brown though. He's a regular dad, a cool guy to hang with. He's the one person you can always go to if you need help or just to shoot the breeze. Ask me why I killed him though.

Yeah, I did shoot him, but like I said, I didn't intend to, not him and not my mom. It just went down that way but it's not how my day started.

For breakfast, my mom fixed her killer jalapeno scrambled eggs and corn bread. After we finished eating, we all sat around, just talking and goofing off.

My mom is the real looker in this family. She has the pale skin that both Devon and I got from her. My mom has gorgeous blue eyes and her hair is a shiny black, natural too. She's slender at five foot six with well toned arms and legs because she swims, does yoga and uses the Stairmaster at home, a few days a week. Devon, my sister, complains a lot about having brown hair and has begged our mom to let her darken it.

Mom never agrees though, telling her she's beautiful without it, and that just makes Dev even more jealous. We razz each other, the four of us, all the time but we're tight. Like I said before, we're family, in every way that counts.

After breakfast, and the usual daily chores, came a soup and sandwich lunch. My mom and Devon went out, separately, to do their own thing. Then it was just Dad and me. He had taken a few days off work to hang with me before I headed off to college.

We nuked some burgers and fries for our dinner, and then hung out in his room, otherwise known by one and all as the "man" cave." Yeah, we have one of those too. It's a place where my dad can go and be alone, or hang with his buddies. Best of all is when I get to hang out there or talk with him about serious stuff. Whatever.

The day I shot my parents was a weekend day like every other one before it. Once the day ended, nothing would ever be the same. Not for anyone.

Like I said, it was just me and my dad sitting in his man cave, cleaning his prized gun collection. For a few hours, it was the way it had always been between us. We kidded around with each other and we talked about what was going on in our lives. It was just another, ordinary day.

In only three short weeks, we'd start loading up the family SUV and taking that long drive up to Massachusetts Institute of Technology (MIT). Most of the conversation between us was about college. We talked a lot about the courses that I would take freshman year. Both of us kind of shook our heads at what they were calling these college courses today.

My Dad and I joked together about the standard line that just about every college and university uses on their websites. You know, it's the one about creating the type of graduate that's going to serve the nation and the world beyond it.

I was more interested in the high rate of employment of their students, since I'd need to get a job once I graduated.

I was just glad that it was my parents paying the tuition. MIT is steep with most of the student body relying on loans and scholarships. However, there's family money that my dad can tap into, and that was his plan for both his kids so that we could have choices. Most of my friends aren't quite that lucky. But even with all the financial help, I still had to hold up my end of things by getting the grades and all.

It was a good thing that I didn't have to declare a major until sophomore year. All I knew for sure was that MIT was the place for me, but the rest? Well, it was early yet and so I passed through the blogs and studied the course listings and that was about it.

Hell, Dad and I even joked a little about the roommate that I had been assigned. There was some laughter and teasing about how I needed to be sure that Alex wasn't short for Alexandra. As I said, things were relaxed between us.

How had it gone so bad so quickly? You hear people talk all the time about how their life changed in a flash. They make a decision like turning left instead of right. On the other hand, maybe it's all about do you take off the seat belt, instead of buckling in.

You make one decision and if it's the wrong one, your life changes forever, or maybe it's just over. If you're like me? You think "Yeah, right." They have too much drama in their life. In reality, it's probably just as boring at times, as the life everyone else has.

They're trying to get that fifteen minutes of fame crap. I swear to you right here and now though that it's true, every single statement. Your life does change and forever and you can't get back yesterday, just like the words in one of my favorite songs. You can't even figure out right away how it went bad so fast.

At least, that's how it was for me. One minute we were united in cleaning the guns, talking and having a good time, and the next I had blurted out the question.

Shock. That's what I saw in my father's eyes, as he slowly lowered the just cleaned colt 45 revolver to the top of his desk.

The minutes dragged on as I waited, with my own hand still on the handle of the gun I was working on. I could feel cold sweat trickling down the back of my t-shirt. Shit, I didn't want to spend today talking about this. I wanted to talk about school, about how nervous I was feeling about being so far from home, but I was going to tough it out. After all, I had brought it up in the first place. The least I could do was wait him out, hear him tell me the truth for once. It's not that he ever lied to me before or at least I never caught him in one.

But you know what? My Dad only had time for a question of his own: "How did you find out?" I forgot that I still held the gun. The minute he asked his question, the gun went off, without my being aware of it. Before I could react, he was slammed back against his chair.

He lay slumped there, the blood gushing from his chest wound. His eyes glazed over, and his movements were slow and unsteady. You want to talk about shock?

If my dad was shocked that he had been shot, how much more stunned did he think I felt? I had fired a gun at my own father! Not just fired but I couldn't seem to make my body move. My hand never even reached towards the cell that sat in front of me. I kept hearing that stupid question my Dad had asked, repeatedly in my head as if it was bouncing off the soundproof walls.

No one really tells you what it's like to kill someone at such close range. Yeah, if I had aimed for his head, I might have watched his face explode.

But I shot him in the chest and it was loud! It was loud, messy, and so final. I never even aimed, the gun just went off. I kept staring at my Dad as I watched the blood pool out of the neat hole I had made dead center in his chest.

All I could think about was wondering if they ever planned to tell Devon and me. Did they think that we'd just never learn the truth, until maybe after both he and Mom were dead? Well, I had taken care of the first part of that and now, I would find out what, if anything, my mother had to say to me.

Somehow, I managed to get my shaky legs up out of the chair, to propel me out of the man cave. Staggering downstairs towards the control panel, I cut off all the electricity to the house, leaving both my cell and my dead father alone.

I slowly climbed back upstairs, holding two guns in my hands. I was armed and I held a full box of ammo. I also had my laptop with me. Guess I thought I could fool around with it while I waited for my mom to come home.

Chapter Two

It was even darker now as I sat back down beside the stairs, reloading the second gun and waiting till my mother returned home. Don't ask me why I thought I needed more than one gun, let alone more ammo. I mean it's not as if I was going out on a killing spree across the neighborhood, or defending my home from a massive invasion. I don't even know why I didn't pick up the phone and call 911. If I had, maybe this wouldn't have been as bad as it turned out.

Can I say in my defense that when you're in shock, you don't think straight? Yeah, it's true. I don't know what I was thinking or even if I was thinking. I just know that one minute I'm staring at my dead father, and the next, I'm sitting on the floor by the stairs. I don't even remember getting there. I sure don't remember taking the guns and ammo with me. I mean, it's not as if I planned on shooting her more than once.

Correction, I wasn't going to shoot her. I was just going to ask her to tell me the truth. Then, I never intended to kill my father either. It was probably better to be prepared, you know, just in case. I kept telling myself to put the guns back.

I needed to call the ambulance, even though I knew that there wasn't anything anyone could do now for my dad. He was too far gone to be helped. I knew that, but I also knew that I didn't have to make any of this worse than it already was.

If I at least put the guns back, then I could talk to my Mom. I could convince her to tell me the truth and she'd help me figure out what to do next.

None of my own words helped though and I kept sitting there, waiting.

Finally, hours later I could hear her key in the lock. I heard the slight pause in her steps as she realized that she wasn't the first one home. Then, I heard the door slowly opening. I saved the file on my laptop and shut it down. Now, no matter what happens, what I know about the secret is locked away.

"Greg? Is anyone here?"

She didn't fumble for the light switch. Her fingers moved unerringly to the exact place on the wall to lift the switch upwards, then down. Knowing my mom, she was frowning as she realized that the power was out. A quick glance out the front door window showed her that our house appeared to be the only one in darkness. She stayed exactly where she was, but now her free hand moved to the front door, as if to open it, to flee.

"I cut the power. Why don't you come on in and answer a question for me?"

It was when I spoke that she knew she hadn't been alone. Still, she stayed right where she was, not moving as her heart beat slowed again, recognizing the voice.

"What are you doing in the dark and what's going on?"

Oh yeah, she was using her "reasonable" voice. The one she used with Dad during those few times that they ever disagreed.

The reasonable voice never worked, but she kept trying anyway. It brought a half grimace of a smile to my face as I remembered, and then I took a deep breath.

"Ok, stay there then. Just answer one question."

The minutes ticked by, seemingly going on and on while I waited for her answer.

....

Numb. That's what I felt when the front door burst open and two armed policemen ran through, their guns at the ready and aimed right at me.

"Drop your weapon. Get on your feet slowly and raise your hands over your head."

The first guy barked out his orders in a voice that made you want to do what he told you to do. Yeah, I think I remember dropping my gun, or maybe it just fell from my fingers. Even now,

I don't really recall which way it happened but I do remember standing up. The rest is a blur to me, almost as if I had been sleepwalking or something. I found myself cuffed and in the back seat of a police cruiser and I don't know what came next. I do know that I sat there for a very long time, waiting.

But what were we waiting for? I think I was wondering how they knew to come in like that. I guess that one of the neighbors heard the shot and called the cops. The caller was probably that Mrs. Pearson from next door.

She's the neighborhood gossip, but an alright kind of lady, kind of old and wrinkly and all of that. Mrs. Pearson's a widow who was always bringing cookies and pies and stuff to the neighbors. She was also the first to know what was going on. It would burn the old lady's ass if she wasn't first with this news, so I kind of hoped that didn't happen. She always had nice things to say to us and I used to mow her lawn and shovel her driveway, until she got a service to take care of things. Sometimes Mrs. Pearson just waved as she was coming or going and we'd all wave back. She kept to herself but she was still a gossip.

I think I sat in that back seat a while. I guessed that they had found my parents because I did hear an ambulance siren in the distance. I even saw the team run into the house, and then they brought them both out all covered up on two gurneys.

By then I was starting to feel tired, so I somewhat just slumped against the window, blowing the hair out of my eyes. I wear it somewhat long, and since my hands weren't free, I didn't have much choice if I wanted to see what was going on. The second cop was sitting in the front seat. He wasn't talking to me. He was just sitting and waiting for his partner.

Once the older looking guy got into the driver's side and started the car, we moved quickly down the street. I kept quiet.

I've watched a lot of cop shows, and that's what they all say you should do. Don't say anything unless it's to ask for a lawyer. We don't have a lawyer, not that it mattered. I'd probably get a public defender. Hey, maybe she'd be some hot young thing, but then I realized that's how they all look on TV and the movies.

In real life, they probably just looked like everyone else, maybe even ugly, not that I cared. I wanted a bed, somewhere to lie down and sleep. I really wanted to start this day all over and do things differently. Would I still have killed my parents, if I knew that this was how my day was going to end? My mom used to talk about stuff like this all the time. Some things are just meant to be. Even if you try, you still end up where you needed to be in the first place, even if the journey takes you longer to get there. Funny the stuff you remember, isn't it?

Chapter Three

The door to Interrogation One pushed open, and a woman who appeared to be in her mid-thirties, stepped in, ID in hand.

"I'm Alice Carrins, Public Defender's Office, assigned to Lucas Fielding."

Beneton turned, nodded in her direction, while secretly cursing his luck to get the terrier of the public defender's office.

Alice Carrins didn't look like a terrier; she looked like a princess. She may not have had that requisite long golden blonde hair; keeping hers in a short pixie cut. Nevertheless, it suited her, highlighting a fine boned and delicately pale skinned face. Alice had deep set, bright blue eyes that could look right through you. She was even short and just curvy enough to be noticed, but that was all on the outside.

What mattered, at least to Alice, was how she felt. She never felt like a princess. She certainly never asked for the scores of hopelessly romantic men to slay her dragons, real or imagined. Alice wanted to do that all by herself. Despite the frustrating fact that she barely topped out at five foot four, she believed that she had the power to do just that.

The problem, as she saw it was that growing up, she couldn't convince anyone to even let her try.

Her parents, John and Lucinda Wolverton Carrins had always dreamed of a little Alice in Wonderland. They were beyond thrilled the day she was born and they did their best to keep young Alice safely cocooned and out of danger.

The primary goal of her parents, as they saw it, was to nurture their precious little girl until she grew up and married into yet another wealthy and influential family.

Their daughter, well, let's just say that she had other plans...

Alice was always top in her classes. She made school valedictorian at seventeen, and was president of the debate club. She was a glee club soloist, not to mention having her own weekly article in the school newspaper. Alice tried out for track and made the team as their top sprinter. She also got a spot on the girl's volleyball team. In the summers, she was a top rated rower. Alice never stopped moving, making sure that all of her pursuits would take her as far away from that "princess" label as possible.

Did it work? Well, she was able to keep most guys away simply by keeping too busy to date through high school. She was so busy, that she ended up missing her prom, which wasn't that big a deal to her.

It bothered her parents, which just made it irresistible, something that completely mystified her parents.

They kept encouraging her to try more "girly" activities. Unfortunately, the more they encouraged, the further away from all of that she went.

Alice knew that her parents meant well. The problem was that they had never understood that she hated looking like a princess. She hated the fact that every guy she came across seemed unwilling or at the very least unable to accept the fact that just because she was small and had such pretty, doll like features, it didn't mean that she needed a champion.

Her troubles had all started back in first grade when a runaway dodge ball from a rowdy fifth grade class at recess had struck Alice in the back, knocking her down into the dirt and ripping her dress. Before she could get to her feet, the entire group of first grade boys had surrounded the older boy. They all demanded that he apologize to Alice and offer to pay for her dress. The girls all applauded, but she had felt her face reddening from severe embarrassment.

From that point on, every time anyone so much as brushed against Alice or accidentally bumped into her, the boys would all jump to her defense. They often ended up fighting with one another to be the one to "save" her.

Alice's life did become progressively easier over time. At least in high school she made one decision where she finally saw eye to eye with her parents. They all agreed that she belonged in one of the two all girl's catholic school, even if they had different reasons for their decision.

Alice chose the one that was located in the downtown area. The location of this school would enable her to continue to pursue her interests of championing the down and out members of society.

It almost didn't happen, but for a chance comment from the principal, that this kind of work activity was part of her class requirements. That's how she won the argument over where to spend her four years of high school.

As far as her parents were concerned, she was allowed to pursue this area of interest as long as there was no interference with her grades.

Things were going along well until her sophomore year, when the high school due to declining enrollment, decided to close. Once more, there were nightly debates on just where she should go next. They all agreed that she had already benefited from the catholic teaching. Instead of being sent to the other all girl's catholic school, Alice was set on attending the first catholic high school in the city to become coeducational since the early seventies.

Once her father learned of that part of things, he was hesitant but she had done her homework. Hours of study at the local library had unearthed the news that the school where she wished to go had established an international baccalaureate program.

This particular program was extremely rigorous. Students had to take several courses. These included foreign languages, math, history, and science.

After students completed the core curriculum, they learned what was called "complete theory of knowledge." In this particular course, students were taught how and what people learn. They then had to compose a 4,000-word essay of independent research in one of the subject areas being studied.

Her choice for a new high school was the only one in this part of the state to offer such a program. It would turn her and the other graduates into better thinkers and writers as well as prepare her for college.

Her father, convinced that he was more of a modern thinker than his own parents, was supportive of his girl going to college. Alice merely saw it as a stepping-stone leading to law school.

Her work with the underprivileged gave her more experience than most, so that she felt more prepared for college, and law school. However, that last goal she kept to herself. She needed her father on her side until he had paid for her high school and college. Law school would have to come at Alice's own expense. Her father, finally convinced, willingly gave his assent and young Alice enrolled for her junior year.

Life in her new high school wasn't much easier with boys insisting on carrying her books, or her cafeteria tray or opening doors for her. Her first few weeks in the new high school had been an almost physical nightmare.

That is until the day during a tug of war over her cafeteria tray, she had simply let go, which caused the tray and all of its contents to splash all over her would be "helper." Alice merely stepped around him, got back in line, and got a new tray sitting down at a table by herself until little by little, several other girls joined her.

They weren't the first string that her father would have wanted her to associate with and that pleased Alice. Nevertheless, what really made her happy was that she had finally found friends, for the first time in her life. These girls would help define her, help her to get more in touch with the "real" her, the one that been struggling against repression for years and now, finally, she felt that she belonged. They were the ones that encouraged her extra curriculum activities, the ones that finally made her see just how capable she truly was.

They also understood her need to get as far away from home as possible upon graduation.

To that end, despite being accepted at four different colleges and universities, she chose Georgetown for her undergraduate pre-law degree and packed up her belongings. Her dorm room provided a safe haven for it was her first time to be truly alone in a different town, without her parents.

Despite their concerns about life in the big city as they called Washington, D.C., they were still pleased that she had chosen a name school.

Alice had made sure to point out some of the more illustrious alumni such as former President Bill Clinton, Maria Shriver and even Patrick Ewing to name a few. Her mother was equally amenable that her daughter chose the nation's oldest Catholic University. They were so pleased, that they barely blinked when they discovered that community service was part of the package, which was required by just about every other college and university.

Again, Alice graduated at the top of her class, spending any and all of her free time studying. It paid off when she had been granted a partial scholarship at Cornell Law School, one of the most demanding and prestigious in the country. Alice had chosen Cornell based solely on the fact that students in the law school were able to get involved in pro bono work early through the public service challenge.

Her father was convinced when he heard through a colleague of his about a five-week program at the Paris Summer Institute.

He didn't explain to his friends and colleagues that his daughter was there training in both comparative and international law. He only mentioned that his daughter was spending time in France for the summer, as he eagerly opened up his checkbook, paying the extra fees without protest. He even paid for her stay in a swanky two-bedroom apartment within walking distance of the school.

Her mother tried to console herself with the hope that her daughter would still find time for husband hunting and kept quiet, not wanting to say or do anything that might push Alice in a different direction altogether.

However, once she graduated at the top of her class from law school, and started to work in the public defenders office, her father grew more approhensive. His only daughter had turned down several lucrative jobs at top ranking law offices and was showing no indication of changing her mind.

All her father could see were the years of potential wasted on a daughter, who still wouldn't be pushed towards the debutante life, and couldn't even see the benefits of aligning herself with a lucrative practice. He had fully expected that she would see the error of her ways and move towards Wall Street or some high-powered local firm instead. How could he possibly explain to his friends and colleagues that his daughter didn't want to leave the public defender's office? What would everyone think?

Her mother was much more upset about the fact that she wasn't married or even engaged, and kept bringing up the subject every time Alice came home for a visit.

The only advantage she had was a refusal to return until they stopped their barrage of questions and continual concerns about how she was wasting her life.

Alice was very stubborn, she had learned from the best on what buttons to push with her parents. Even though she felt a little guilty about having to manipulate them, she kept telling herself that this was just how her family operated. At least they had never come to see Alice and the sparsely decorated apartment in a not too good part of town. That would probably have killed them, or at the very least sent them into panic mode where they might end up hiring private security guards, none of which she wanted. She could be grateful for that at least.

Chapter Four

"Alice."

She blinked a little, feeling distracted and swiftly refocused, turning towards the detective who was giving her one of those looks, the one that said he knew she'd been daydreaming.

"Has my client said anything to you?"

It was the first few minutes that determined most of the outcomes and minors were easy jjpickings, especially to a seasoned vet like Beneton but the guy only shook his head.

"Not one word. You might have better luck."

He got to his feet and opened the door, pausing with his hand on the doorknob.

"Oh, yeah, the kid turned eighteen today, so guess you're dealing with an adult."

With that announcement, he walked out, closing the door behind him, leaving her and her client alone.

Alice nodded thanks and moved quickly to sit down across from Lucas in the chair that the detective had just vacated.

The boy looked up, briefly, met her eyes with green eyes that held no emotion, not even remorse in them. This wasn't going to be a walk in the park, not for either side.

"I'm Alice Carrins and I've been assigned as your public defender, Lucas. Now before you get too chatty with me, let me explain a few things. First, you don't have to say anything, not one word but it will be easier to prepare your defense if you cooperate with me. In order to help me do my job, you only answer what I ask you. You don't volunteer anything more, you got that?"

She waited to see if he would talk, and when he continued staring at her, she shook her own head.

"Lucas, nod your head if you understand."

He nodded his head slowly and she continued.

"Ok, now. Do you remember having your rights read to you?"

Lucas nodded his head.

"Good. Do you understand those rights?"

He nodded again.

"Alright, now, let's get down to it."

I turned towards the voice and blinked a little. Man, oh man, did I ever hit the jackpot! This woman was hot alright, short and curvy all over. I kept my thoughts to myself, and tried to keep my reaction from my face, just to be sure. The detective that had tried grilling me for hours didn't look all that happy to see her, but I couldn't wait to be alone with her.

Hey, I'm eighteen after all and you know what they say about sex and death and all of that, right? Not that I had much chance of that happening, but a guy can dream, can't he? I waited till it was just us in that room and let her talk first.

She might be a hot looking older blonde but she knew how to do her job. She explained that I didn't have to volunteer anything, I just had to answer her questions and that I could handle. Once she started talking though, I started to actually listen and pretty soon I almost forgot what she looked like. I mean, yeah, I kept glancing up at her and all, and she was still hot in that whole Mrs. Robinson thing, not that I had any experience hooking up with someone that much older. I don't know how to explain it. I just know that once she got going, I didn't care about her looks.

"You know Lucas, I like a challenge as much as the next lawyer, and your case is proving to be one for the books. Now, if you had stopped at shooting your Dad?" Alice shrugged her shoulders slightly. "I could get you off on accidental death and we'd be done. A few days, weeks at most and you'd be a free man.

Instead, our crime unit puts you at the scene of the crime, your prints all over the murder weapon, which you then use on your mother."

Alice waited to let that sit in, figuring I guess that it would make me squirm and man, did I ever want to but I'm not stupid. I'm going to MIT in a few weeks, they even gave me a scholarship so I kept my eyes on her face and my mouth shut.

"You waited more than two hours for your mother to come home and then you shot her. Then you stayed in the house after the first phone call from a neighbor went through to 911. You didn't even make any effort to flee the scene." She paused before adding, "Did your parents hit you or your sister?"

Silence from me. "Did they sexually assault either one of you?"

I tried to leap out of the chair but those chains held me tight in my seat.

"What the hell? No, they didn't sexually assault us, and no they didn't hit us either. Why would you ask about that? Do I look like someone who's been sexually assaulted?"

Alice allowed herself a brief softening of her lips but it wasn't quite a smile as she continued.

"Your parents never beat you, never assaulted you or your sister. How am I supposed to come up with a defense when you don't give me anything to work with?"

I just shrugged a little too. You told me not to talk so what do you expect? Ok, yeah, I did talk but shit, I wasn't going to keep quiet when she was bringing that stuff up. I didn't have much to say even though it really pissed me off when she asked about the whole sexual assault shit. I mean, come on, ask anyone, we're or were the all American family. Ask the neighbors if you don't believe me. Ask.... My head snapped up as I remembered that you couldn't ask dead people anything.

She waited for him to calm down and then she continued.

"I sent Price out to canvass the neighborhood. Maybe he'll find something you don't want me to know that will work for us. Otherwise, this is going to take every talent I have to keep you out of jail. You do realize that Pennsylvania has the death penalty right? You're legally an adult. We don't have any loophole either since you were already an adult when you killed your parents." She paused to let that sink in before continuing. "I don't know what you expect me to do, Lucas. Let's just hope that Price gets lucky."

Price? Who the hell is Price? Was Price the bodyguard or some errand boy? Guess I'll find out as I just sat there, keeping my mouth shut and my ears open.

Yeah, I get that I could fry in the chair for the double murder stuff but you're good, right? I mean, I saw that look on the old detective's face. He didn't look happy to see you and that tells me that you're really good.

35

Chapter Five

Earlier in the evening........

Since there were police cars everywhere, Devon was forced to park her used car at the corner of the block. She grabbed her purse, locked up and set out on foot. At least it wasn't cold out, it was still late summer and she was wearing sneakers, her hands shoved deep into the pockets of her coat. Devon pushed back the hood. Her brown hair spilled messily out of the ponytail she had loosely shoved it into on her way home.

The first police cruiser had an officer standing next to it, so she coughed a little just to get his attention.

"What's going on?" She shifted from foot to foot, while biting down on her lower lip. What was going on that the cops were in her neighborhood? Was someone shot?

"Miss, you should be inside. We have a situation and you don't want to be here. Go on home now."

He turned back, dismissing her and she coughed again.

"Um, yeah, but here's the thing, I kinda live down there."

She pointed towards the other end of the block where she could see even more police cruisers parked and a growing crowd of neighbors.

Whatever was going on, Devon knew it had to be big, if the size of that crowd was any indication. She stole a quick glance at her watch and started to fidget a little.

Great, this was all she needed on top of everything else tonight. It was about five minutes to eleven and she had what her mother called a "Cinderella" license. That meant that she could only drive until eleven o'clock. Well, at least Devon was with the police and it wasn't her fault that she was standing here, instead of being already in her own home, where she was supposed to be, right?

"Hold on, Miss. What's your house number?"

He had his hand on the radio, ready to call it.

"4201 is the white two stories on the left, with the big oak tree out in front."

He didn't seem to react as he called it in.

"I need an officer here at the corner. Got a young woman here, claims to live in 4201. "

He opened the back of the squad car, motioned for her to get inside and she slipped in, her hands starting to shake. This was sounding worse with every passing moment as she sat down, wrapping her arms around her waist.

Her mother always took pride in the fact that Devon had a good head on her shoulders, but right now, she felt even younger than sixteen. All she wanted was her mom.

It was never good when the cops wouldn't answer your questions and kept you in their squad car. Lucas had taught her that from all those cop shows he was always watching.

All Devon could do now was wait but she had questions too and she was going to ask and ask until someone answered her.

....

Alice knew that there was no such thing as a coincidence, but she still thought herself lucky to be at the right place, at the right time even if that time and place happened to be a murder scene.

It was right after work and she was still dressed in her serviceable navy suit with sensible three-inch black pumps. The black pumps were what she called her power shoes because they added enough height so that people didn't automatically try and ignore her. Her bulging briefcase still sat in the passenger side of her six-year-old Honda Accord.

She made the turn onto 5th and Central, when she saw the police cars. Carefully, she parked on the side of the road and got out, flashing her ID to the officer that turned around to face her.

"Alice Carrins, Public Defender's Office. What's going on?"

He told her, briefly, at least as much as he knew and jerked a thumb towards his back seat. As she peered around his left shoulder, Alice saw what appeared to be a female, minor, looking terrified.

"Is she a witness?"

The officer, Drew Tarryton shook his head.

"The killer's sister. We'll be taking her downtown in a few minutes, once we've secured the scene."

Alice nodded and pulled out her phone, hitting a number and waiting to be connected.

"Serena, this is Alice. Let Price know that I've got another case. I'll be in touch when I know more."

Disconnecting the call, she shoved her phone back into the pocket of her black leather coat and waited, knowing that she didn't want to be too far behind once things started moving.

Chapter Six

Back to the present...

"Is there anyone you want us to contact, Lucas?"

"Devon."

She paused, put her iPad down, and looked up at me.

"Who's Devon?"

"Devon is my little sister."

There was an even longer pause as Alice just stared, hard, into my eyes. Man, she was good. I felt it like she had reached out and actually touched me and all she did was look. Ok, Ok, maybe I squirmed a little but geez, the woman was tough and she was starting to break through that numbness that I had wrapped around me ever since my butt first hit that police car's back seat.

"Where is Devon, Lucas?"

How the hell should I know where she was? I may have remembered her but I wasn't in charge of what she... Oh yeah, I did know, well kinda.

I shrugged my shoulders a little.

"It's Wednesday, or at least it was. I don't know, she should have tried to come home by now." That's when I realized something. Where exactly **was** my sister?

"Lucas, if your sister was on her way home when all of this went down? She's probably in protective custody. Let me check on that for you. For the record, it's now Thursday morning."

She slid her chair back and grabbing her pad, shoved it into her bag before heading out the door, shutting it behind her.

I saw the face of the prison guard and shook my head. How far do you think I'm going to get? My hands might be free but my left leg was still cuffed to the table. It's not like I'm MacGyver or anything so yeah, I just sat there and waited....

....

"You're looking for Lucas' sister. That's right. The name is Devon and she's a minor. I want her found and brought down here. Yeah, Price, I get that it's after two in the morning and yeah, yeah. Ok, yeah, you're right." She paused, rubbing her forehead a little. Alice was starting to feel tired. "In that case, I want to talk to whoever took Devon into protective custody. Yeah, I want her woken up."

She hung up her phone and just let out a breath. It was Price's job to make the call and find the sister. It was Alice's job to talk to her and find out what, if anything was said to the cops. If Devon was as close mouthed as her brother was, well, Alice might get lucky there.

If Devon said anything, it was more likely a denial of why her brother had killed their parents, but Alice had done this job long enough to know that you don't leave anything to fate. If there was information to be gathered from this source, then that's exactly what she was going to do.

She paced the small hallway, even grabbed a decent cup of coffee, and stood, sipping it until her phone buzzed.

"This is Alice Carrins. Yes, Melissa, good to hear from you as well, glad that you're on the case. How's Devon? Uh huh. Good, and yes, I agree, that she needs her rest. I'm going to want to talk to her first thing tomorrow. Yes, I know but it's my job."

She chuckled softly at the other woman's protests that the girl was only sixteen, that she was beyond shocked to find herself in this nightmare and that she needed protecting until it was all over.

"Have you contacted any next of kin? Yes, I know she has a brother but I don't think the state is going to look all that kindly on a suspected double murderer taking on that responsibility, do you? That's right and yes, nine tomorrow, Melissa. Of course, I understand that you'll be with her. I would expect nothing less. Good night."

Ok, that worked.

She took one last gulp of her coffee, crushing the paper cup and tossing it neatly into the nearest can before walking back down the hall and into the room again.

Chapter Seven

It was the middle of a beautiful dream, one Sylvie hadn't experienced in a very long time, and it was so real to her. Her body stretched luxuriantly under the heavy covers in the big, king-sized bed.

In the dream, she was wearing a ridiculous excuse for a bikini and lying on a white, sandy beach. The waves were lapping gently on the shore; her newly painted toes were dancing to the reggae beat that was piping through the headphones on her iPod.

There was a small collapsible table beside her that held a long, cool, tropical drink made up of coconut, mango, rum, fruit juice, and topped by one of those silly umbrellas.

At first, the insistent buzzing had her flicking her hand impatiently at what was surely a most annoying bee. The flicking fingers did nothing though to stop that constant buzzing, which was growing louder by the minute. Suddenly, the sun became completely blocked from view by a broad figure whose large hands gripped her shoulders, shaking her and calling her by name.

"Sylvie, wake up."

"What's going on?"

Her voice sounded sluggish, even to her own ears as she struggled, caught between her desire to just stay there on that sunny beach, lulled by the gentle, warm breeze and to the pressing need to wake up, like the voice commanded. Strange, but it sounded like her husband.

In the end, the shaking did the trick and she woke, just a little, but then she was never very good in the morning hours, at least not before she had her coffee.

Sylvie opened her eyes, confused as she stared straight up into the irritated blue eyes of her husband, Brad. He released her, flipping on the bedside lamp and handed her a cup of coffee. Grateful, she began to sip while sitting up, watching as Brad yanked on a pair of blue jeans and a blue sweater.

"Come on, we have to get to the airport. I'll get the bags, and you can pack what you think you'll need for a few days."

With that, Brad slipped on his loafers and going to the closet, pulled out a matching pair of suitcases. Putting both on the foot of the bed, he went over to the chest of drawers and began to yank out his clothing, neatly packing and clearly expecting Sylvie to do the same.

Once she had finished the coffee and was starting to feel more human, only then did she ask the first of the myriad of questions that had bombarded her consciousness.

Brad seemed to understand that Sylvie felt a little strange to find that she was not on that hot, sandy beach from her dream. Instead, she had awoken to find herself in her own bed in the small town in Montana, blinking to try to bring herself to full awakening.

"What's this about the airport? What's going on? Where are we?" She glanced at the alarm clock and wiped her eyes.

"It's barely five in the morning. All I remember is having a great dream until some buzzing bee interrupted it and then there you were shaking me awake."

"That buzzing sound was the phone. Some woman named Melissa from Protective Services in Erie, Pennsylvania. I didn't get all the details, just that something terrible happened earlier to Greg and Susanna. The most important thing is that we need to get there as soon as we can.

I texted Patty, woke her up too and she's already started trying to figure out a flight plan that will get us out there. She suggested that we just get to the airport as quickly as we can and let her handle the rest.

Come on, Sylvie. You barely have enough time to pack and then we're out of here."

Sylvie nodded and got out of bed, hurriedly packing her own things. She picked up her iPhone, intending to call Glenda, their next-door neighbor. The woman was a morning person, although she probably would be waking her up, but she was the most helpful person that Sylvie knew.

Seconds before pressing the last number, it all finally sank in and she whirled slowly around, facing her husband.

"Were Susanna and Greg in an accident? What about Lucas and Devon?'

Patiently, because he understood that no matter how hard she tried, his wife would never be a morning person, Brad came over to where Sylvie stood and gently put a hand on her shoulder.

"They're dead, Sylvie. I don't know how it happened. I just know that Devon is in protective custody and they need us there as soon as we can manage it."

There was a beep on his phone, signaling an incoming text and he looked down, shaking his head a little.

"Ok, Patty has us booked on the next flight out which leaves at 7:35. If we hurry, we might be able to grab a donut at the airport. Call Glenda from your phone in the cab, Sylvie. We don't have any more time."

"They're dead? What? What are you talking about?"

Brad sighed, frustrated.

"Look, I know as much as you do and we don't have time for this. Come on, we have to take the bags downstairs, so we can get out of here on time."

As he was talking, he was guiding Sylvie and her bag out of the bedroom, and down the stairs, hoping that the taxi he had texted for would be on time.

The call had come in early enough but it took forever to wake his wife, something he had told this Melissa person. It was going to be a long flight with two connections, but they would get there and get things sorted out.

He would need to make hotel reservations too, Brad thought absently, as he heard the first honking of a horn. Sylvie had managed to grab her purse that held her phone with one hand while the other hand held the suitcase.

It was a carry on like her husband's so Sylvie knew that should help them in this mad dash out of the house. She got into the back seat of the taxi, letting Brad handle the two suitcases and telling the driver to get them to the airport as quickly as possible. Once he had joined her in the back, Brad went right to work locating a hotel that would be close enough to the local jail and booking them a room for an indefinite time.

The driver had the radio on, set to easy rock, which just helped get him into work mode. A quick look over at his wife reassured him that Sylvie was texting Glenda instead of talking to

49

her. He didn't want the driver to know how long they planned on being gone.

Sylvie for her part had an ongoing dialogue in texts between herself and Glenda, asking the older woman if she would handle the mail and paper and the watering and care of her plants. She was grateful that the other woman quickly agreed to help, never once asking what was going on. What Sylvie couldn't have known was that the local news had already picked up the story and Glenda had seen it on the TV while she was eating her oatmeal and toast. The double homicide didn't look good for Lucas, but Glenda wasn't about to update Sylvie, not with the long flight they had ahead of them.

Once she was finished confirming things, Sylvie ended her call and looked over at Brad, wondering which one of them should try to contact his father.

Harrison Fielding, a former county council member, was a very busy man, both business wise and politically.

He had many powerful friends and other connections that could be helpful in this kind of situation. Whatever happened, Harrison was the one to go to for help. Sylvie knew that he didn't suffer fools greatly. Before she or Brad made that call, they needed more answers than questions.

Chapter Eight
In a private office suite in Chicago...

"Mr. Fielding, the latest is coming across the screen right now."

Harrison looked up from his morning paperwork to study the TV that was already broadcasting what little they knew of his son and daughter-in-law.

"Greg Fielding, forty and his wife, thirty eight years old Susanna Fielding were found shot to death in their home in Millcreek Township. Their son, eighteen year old, Lucas Fielding, has been taken in for questioning. At this time, the rest of the details remain in the tight-lipped control of the local police. We do know that a 45-colt revolver was recovered at the scene, having appeared to be used, perhaps as the murder weapon.

CSI teams have been swarming around the home collecting evidence, but so far, we have been unable to get any more information as to what, if anything has been found.

We will keep you posted as details become available. This is Lindsey Faith, WICU News. Back to you, Dave."

Harrison turned down the TV again, frowning.

"No one thought to mention Devon."

"Um, Mr. Fielding?"

His secretary, Ruth, a slightly overweight woman in her thirties, waited for more information. She had held this position for over five years and knew how fortunate she was, even though Mr. Fielding was frequently snapping out directives and expecting miracles.

Ruth knew how Harrison felt about exercise and that his diet was carefully regulated. That just made her crave her fast food even more. However, Ruth got results, and in the world that Harrison Fielding inhabited, that was all that truly mattered. Besides, he didn't have much spare time in his daily schedule to spend much of it worrying about the health habits of any of those that worked for him and for that, she was lucky.

Impatient as was his usual nature, Harrison got to his feet, his long, rangy frame of 6'5", flexing, as he gave himself one slow stretch of muscles barely contained beneath the double breasted suit he habitually wore to work.

For a man of his age, Harrison was in remarkably excellent health. At sixty-four, he was in the best shape thanks to his daily workouts and healthy meals. His dark brown hair was expertly styled and his green eyes still sparkled with youth.

"I need you to find out where Devon, my granddaughter, is, Ruth. Do it as discreetly as possible and book me on the next flight to Erie.

Have James throw a bag together for me and meet me at the airport. Cancel all my appointments and commitments until further notice."

"Of course, Mr. Fielding."

Brisk and professional, Ruth scribbled down his systematic instructions and hurriedly moved from the room. She shot a text to James, Mr. Fielding's personal assistant, and then contacted the airlines. By the time her employer was downstairs in his town car, he had a texted message of which flight would be taking him nonstop from the airport to Erie International Airport. Using the pre-arranged payment plan, used for all of his business and professional travel, his ticket would be waiting for him.

James would also be there. He had made the most of his time in packing what he believed that Harrison would need, having worked for him for over ten years now. He got into his own VW Jetta and drove quickly to the airport, hoping that he would get there first.

If there was one thing James had learned in all these years, it was that Harrison Fielding waited for no one. James had managed a quick coffee and a donut. He took his last bite just as Harrison strode down the passageway towards him.

Tossing the finished napkin and empty cup into the nearest trash can, James got to his feet, handing the ticket to Harrison. He held onto the suitcase, which would be loaded onto the plane as soon as the man was on his way to the tarmac. James was a slight man in his forties, with a noticeable comb over from early balding. He knew better than to be caught eating or drinking on the job. His boss thought such habits showed laziness and James liked his job too much to jeopardize it. He was lucky that he was already at Harrison's home office when Ruth called. Being an early riser, James frequently was at work at least ten minutes before he was scheduled and today that habit was very helpful.

The airport was no more than a ten-minute quick ride, which he managed in just fewer than six.

"Good morning, Sir. Your flight is scheduled to leave on time at 9:24 a.m., to arrive in Erie by 10:54 a.m. I took the liberty of renting a car and driver to take you from the airport."

As he spoke, the two men were heading for the prepaid lines and James was handing over the needed paperwork."

"Excellent, James and yes, I would prefer a car and driver. What hotel have you booked for me?"

"The Inn on the Bay has a most excellent reputation and is merely a ten minute drive from there to the jail, Sir. If you wish, I can finalize the room for you."

He held up his phone to show the text. All he had to do was press the button and the room would be rented.

Harrison nodded agreeably.

"Do that James and let Ruth know that I'll be in touch once I set down in Erie. I'll call you as well."

James merely nodded, as he handed over the suitcase. He waited until the plane had taxied out to the end of the runway.

Once it made the air, James left the airport and took himself back to Harrison's home, to continue to do his work and to wait for the man's call.

Chapter Nine

Alice sat back down, making a show of putting her things back on the table, while she studied the young man who was sitting across from her. It was now nearing three a.m. and he didn't look as exhausted as he must have felt.

"Lucas, we found your sister. She's in protective custody, spending the night at a safe house. Devon will be here tomorrow morning and you can talk to her after I do.
Try and get some sleep and I'll talk to you then. I need my own bed."

He nodded his head, looking tired now and young. That image stayed with her as she let herself out of the room, confirming the arrangements with the officer outside.

Once that was completed, she moved briskly down the hall, taking the stairs because they were faster. She got into her small, blue compact and headed to the apartment building five blocks away. It wasn't the best of neighborhoods, but it was safe enough, and the security on the place was just a bit above average.

Alice parked in the closed lot, always checking her surroundings, and headed inside.

It didn't take long to wash off her makeup, brush her teeth and use the toilet, before she undressed, pulled back the faded comforter and making sure that her alarm was set, crawled into bed. She willed herself to sleep, hoping to get at least three good hours before her day would start all over again.

Ok, they found Devon. That was good, right? Protective custody meant that she was in good hands and I'd get to see her and talk to her, tomorrow.

What could she be thinking? How was I ever going to explain this to her? I mean, she's still just a kid, even if she does have a driver's license.

The officer came in after Alice left, uncuffing me from the table, and then leading me down a series of hallways. I stumbled a few times and he helped me find my feet. Sorry but I'm kinda tired here. I didn't want to cause any more trouble, so I did my best to walk straight. Some officers, this one at least, had been half-decent to me, calling me by my first name and treating me like a person, not like some crazed mad man that gunned down my own parents.

Did any of them think I would have killed Devon too if she had been home? As if. I mean, yeah, she's annoying most of the time and completely boy crazy and all of that but she's my little sister. I would kill for her, not kill her.

But then, I never saw myself as the kind of guy who would kill my parents either so who knows, right? I climbed into the bed and pulled the blanket up around me.

57

If I had thought about it, I would have picked some worn out jeans or something. Instead, I chose one of my favorite T-shirts; so of course, they were going to test those. Isn't that what they do in crime stories? Now I'm starring in my own and it's nothing like I thought it would be.

I got a bed tonight even if it was a holding cell but the mattress wasn't bad and the sheets seemed clean enough. It was a good thing I was lying down though because I couldn't help but feel my body jerk when the door closed shut, locking me in.

I just kept my eyes closed, turned to the wall, and tried to fall asleep....

....

There was fresh fruit on the center of the kitchen island and Melissa was standing at the stove, cooking something. Devon sniffed a little, and just smiled wanly. From the combination of smells as well as looking over at the older woman, she could tell that they would be eating scrambled eggs and bacon.

"Morning."

Melissa turned around, a smile on her face that was supposed to make Devon feel better but if anything, she felt worse. She had spent a night tossing and turning in a room that wasn't her own, in a house that she had never seen before and now a woman she barely knew, was fixing her breakfast, trying to make her feel better.

Devon wanted her mother, desperately wanted to see her and her father and she started to cry, knowing that would never happen again. Melissa quickly turned off the stove and came over to wrap her arms around her, just holding the girl and letting her sob into her shoulder.

It was better that she let it out a little. The girl had been strangely silent all the way here last night...

"I'm Ok, thanks." Devon backed out of Melissa's arms and sniffed a little as the woman reached for a box of Kleenex sitting on the table.

"Here, these should help. Why don't you sit down and I'll fix your plate.

You're going to need to eat, even if you don't think you can, Devon. It's going to be a very long day for you, but I'll be with you, to see you through it all."

Before Devon could protest, she found herself seated at the island on one of the dark cherry stools, a platter piled high with bacon and eggs, with a glass of fruit juice in front of her.

Melissa had fixed a plate for herself along with a hot cup of coffee and she sat down, companionably across from Devon and dug in.

Incredibly, Devon felt some hunger and put one strip of bacon along with a handful of eggs on her plate, saying little, and oddly, feeling a little comforted, both by the food and by the older woman.

"So, you like, do this as a job?" She swallowed before asking her question, curious now and hoping not to talk about her brother, at least, not yet.

Melissa nodded as she responded.

"Yes, this is what I do. I'm a care giver for people that need a place to stay, a friendly support and I'm also the person that stands up for those who need it."

She fixed dark brown eyes upon the girl with the tousled brown hair and green eyes.

Devon was wearing a pair of faded blue jeans along with a blue T-shirt, both borrowed. The girl's face was freshly scrubbed without any makeup and curiously enough, she hadn't even asked for any.

The police had confiscated her purse, but since she wasn't a suspect or an accomplice, they had left her clothes alone. She'd get the purse back today.

Without makeup, Devon looked even younger than her sixteen years, and Melissa felt a wave of compassion sweep over her. Life as she knew it would never be the same again.

As she helped herself to another small serving of eggs, Devon tried to sound friendly even though she still felt strange and alone.

"So, like, how did you get into this kind of work?"

Melissa poured herself a cup of coffee, noticing with a slight frown the small amount of food that the girl still had on her plate. Maybe she wasn't a morning person but she thought that it was more likely a result of feeling out of place.

"I was a foster care child when I was little, was bounced around a lot, and learned quickly how to handle myself so that I wouldn't be considered trouble.

I guess it stuck with me that I could bring that experience to the job and I just knew when I first started that this was the right path."

Devon nodded a little, getting it.

"I don't have a clue what I want to do yet and I know that I have two more years in school, so I kinda need to think about it a little more. You know?"

Melissa did know. Devon would have a lot more on her plate than merely deciding on a future, but it wasn't up to Melissa to talk about any of that.

She was here to keep Devon safe, to let her cry it out or throw tantrums, whatever she needed to do. Melissa was also responsible for providing necessary transport. The rest would have to be up to the family that was left and whatever therapist or counselor would be assigned to her.

Melissa had seen difficult cases before. This wasn't all that different, but she didn't intend to burn out so she kept herself somewhat removed emotionally. She had her own future to take care of and she fully intended to get a pension. Melissa had a half dozen more years ahead of her at least.

"Devon, we need to get going. I'll need to call your aunt and uncle and let them know what's going on so that they can come and be here for you."

"But, I thought...." Confusion was written all over the teenager's face until it seemed to dawn on her just what Melissa was saying.

If her parents were dead, and her brother was in jail, then she needed a guardian and for that, her aunt and uncle had to step in. Both Lucas and Devon had known that Uncle Brad and Aunt Sylvie were legal guardians should anything happen to their parents.

Devon was glad that she wasn't the one to have to break the news and wondered just how her aunt and uncle were going to react.

"You don't think they're going to be mad, do you? I mean at Lucas."

They had worked together on cleaning up the dishes and the kitchen with Devon doing her best to be helpful and not a problem.

"I don't know but they're not going to blame you, Devon. If your parents took the time and attention needed to select them as guardians, then they'll come here for you. Don't worry, I've dealt with families like this before, and I'll help you to work through this tough time.

Now, let's get going, we have an appointment with the public defender that's been assigned to your brother's case." Melissa sounded reassuring, but Devon wasn't quite so sure. She just nodded, as if she understood but there wasn't anything about this that made sense to her.

She slipped on the same light coat and sneakers she had worn last night, then followed Melissa outside where the car was parked.

Chapter Ten

Price had talked to every neighbor that would open his or her door. He even went so far as to check the family out via the internet. However, it was always the same story. The picture painted here was that of a loving couple with two great kids who spent a lot of time together, who loved each other and were the "model" family.

There wasn't even a whiff of scandal; no one was having an affair, no drugs, there were no drinking problems. He couldn't find anything wrong with the family. So, what happened to change everything? If this kid was part of the model family, why was he sitting in a conference room, waiting for his public defender? Why had he been charged with two counts of murder?

It wasn't adding up for Alice, it wasn't making any sense at all and she liked when things made sense even if she didn't agree with the answers. Therefore, she walked into the room the next morning, with a cup of coffee in one hand and a chocolate donut in the other. Closing the door behind her, Alice put the donut on a napkin in front of the boy as she sat down across from him.

"The story I keep hearing is that you're part of one big, happy family. The kind that takes vacations, plays sports and games together, and talks things out."

She paused, taking a sip of her coffee while she watched Lucas wolf down his donut.

The kid had just finished eating breakfast but in her world, eighteen was still a kid and kids were always hungry, especially boys.

He just shrugged his shoulders so she shook her head.

"Lucas, you can answer questions that I ask; you just can't add more details. Are we straight on that?"

He finished eating and wiped his mouth, hand reaching for the water glass that was sitting in front of him.

"Yeah, I guess we are. What do you want to know?"

"I want to know what happened, what changed things from this wonderful family that people envied, why you're here in the first place. I mean, your father could easily have been accidental but you stuck around for your mother to come home.

You had to have known everyone's schedule. You live in a good family like yours and you all know what the others are doing, where they are at all times, when to expect them home, that kind of thing. So, what was your plan if your sister got home before your mother? "

She paused again, this time watching him, waiting for a reaction.

"Were you going to kill her too?"

His response was swift and instinctual as he struggled against the cuffs that held him in place, his face reddening with barely contained fury, spitting out his answer.

"You bitch! Do you really think I'd ever in a million years hurt my little sister?"

She shrugged her own shoulders, leaning back in her seat, thankful for the cuffs, but it was what she expected from him and strangely enough, made her feel better about this case.

"Alright, so does this mean that you intended to kill your parents?"

"No! Is that what you really think? You're supposed to be on my side and yet here you are, accusing me of wanting to do away with my parents, my sister."

Alice fought back the smile, knowing he wouldn't be at all understanding if he had seen it on her face.

"I **am** on your side, and you haven't been all that forthcoming, Lucas. Maybe that will change once..."

The persistent knocking had Alice frowning as it interrupted her thoughts, making her stand up to open the door.

Price was standing there and just out of Lucas' view, stood a young girl with an older woman next to her in a protective stance. Alice turned back to Lucas.

"This won't take long. I'll be right back."

Closing the door behind her as she stepped out, she let Price make the introductions.

"Alice, you already know Melissa Daniels, from Protective Services. This is Devon, Lucas' sister."

Alice shook hands with Melissa and offered a hand to Devon. For a moment, the girl held back until Melissa provided some gentle prodding, including a murmured, "It's alright, she's working to help your brother." The whisper seemed to work as Devon shook hands with Alice quickly and then stuck her hand back in her coat pocket.

Alice's first impression was that Devon was a pretty girl, rather slight build but toned, which fit the athletic description of the neighbors. Her long brown hair had a glossy sheen to it and it was well cared for, brushing her shoulders with a slight flip at the ends and parted down the middle of her forehead.

"Can I see Lucas?"

Her voice was soft but more as if she were struggling to hold back tears and Alice just opened the door for the girl, turning to look over at Lucas as she did so.

"Remember, Lucas, you're not to tell Devon anything about what happened."

Alice then shut the door and stepped away; moving down the hall to talk to Melissa; to get the general feel for how things were going with the sister.

....

"Hey, Dev, how are you holding up?"

I tried to sound casual but I could tell that she'd been crying. Geez, I didn't want to have to see her like this, acting so brave as she slowly sat down in the chair across from me, her hands nervously playing with the strings on her coat.

She sat in that hard chair, looking over at me as she wiped her nose with a Kleenex from her pocket. Then she stared right at me, as if willing me to make all of this just goes away. As if I could. I told you that I never planned it out, remember?

"I'm fine, I guess. Melissa, that's the woman from Protective Services? Well, Melissa has been taking good care of me. I even slept a little last night and I ate this morning."

I narrowed my eyes, listening to her talk and wondering what I could say back, since Alice had given me strict instructions not to talk about the case. I had a good feeling that she wasn't someone I wanted angry at me, so I searched around for a safer subject.

"Didn't they let you keep Aloysius with you at least?"

Just the name of that well loved teddy bear made her smile a little and that was a relief. My little sister was the sweetest girl in the world but she had spirit too and I wanted to see some of that, any of that, actually so if bringing up the bear would do it? Yeah, it always made us both smile.

She shook her head though.

"I wish. I haven't been allowed back in the house to get any of my stuff. Melissa can't even go there for a day or two, so I'm wearing borrowed clothes and the police even have my iPod."

She didn't have a cell phone since our parents didn't allow that until she was older but Aloysius?

"Come on, they won't even let you have your bear? What kind of craziness is that? You love that bear, he's been with you like forever."

Aloysius the bear sat in the old rocker in her room, keeping guard over her as she slept. It was where he stayed once she outgrew the need to sleep with him every night. A close friend of her mother's, who had shared the same love for the classic Evelyn Waugh novel; Brideshead Revisited, had given the bear as a gift. Devon had been six months old. The stuffed bear not only fit the description of the bear in the book by being rather large, but both women decided that he be named Aloysius. It was a mouthful for any kid.

It took years of work before Devon could manage anything more than what sounded like "Suss, suss." But it made her smile and Lucas was sure she was remembering some happier days.

"I know but Melissa told me that I should be able to go back there in another day or two and the first thing I'm going for is that bear. You wait and see! "

She leaned forward suddenly, sliding her hands up towards his without touching him.

"Are you alright, Lucas?"

Maybe she had visions of lecherous old men trying to have their way with me in the dark. Maybe it was just seeing me cuffed like this that made her ask, but that was Devon. She was always sweet like this. She was always thinking of other people and here I go and ruin her life forever. I nodded.

"Yeah, yeah, I'm fine. Alice is really good at her job, so this won't be as terrible as it looks."

I know what terrible looks like. I've read enough books, and seen enough movies to know that when you kill two people in the same house, they don't let you walk away.

Alice might be trying to get an insanity plea going. That would mean I'd spend years locked up with a bunch of nuts, but how bad could that be?

I never heard of any insane people trying to take swings at each other in the middle of the night.

"Why did you do it?"

Devon's soft voice pricked at my conscience. How could I possibly explain this? Hell, I didn't even understand and yet I had to tell her something. It was a good thing that I couldn't really answer her question.

"Devon, I can't answer you. You know that, right? I'm not allowed to talk about the case."

She nodded, though I don't think she really understood. It's a lot for a person to take in; I'm having trouble with it myself.

"I know that's what your lawyer said but how could you do it? How could you kill both Mom and Dad? "

71

Devon was trying desperately to figure out what could have possessed her brother to pick up a gun and murder their parents. It left her as a ward of the state, at least until their aunt and uncle got here.

She also knew enough to realize that no matter what happened, she wouldn't be seeing her brother, alone, again for a very long time.

She wasn't angry yet, but that would come in time, and I was thankful for that at least. I could handle anything except seeing Devon angry. For now, the confusion in her eyes was more than I could stand.

Then the door opened and Alice and Melissa both stood there.

"Sorry to have to cut things short but Lucas needs to go back to his cell and change. His arraignment is in thirty minutes."

That was Alice for you, right on schedule and making sure that I knew what to expect. She had gone over what was going to happen at the arraignment.

Alice had also taken my measurements. She sent Price out to buy me a set of new clothes, and a pair of new shoes for the court.

While the guard came in to remove the cuffs from the table, recuffing my hands behind my back for the walk down to the holding cell, I made sure to catch my sister's eye.

"Dev, make sure that they let you get Aloysius and the book too, alright? I always did like Sebastian but don't worry, I'm stronger than he ever was. I love you, sis. You'll **always** be my sister, no matter what, Ok?"

The guard and Alice walked me down to the holding cell, undoing my cuffs and shutting the door behind me so that I could get dressed.

I had just enough time.

....

Devon was more than a little confused at what Lucas had said. Ok, she got that part about the bear. It might sound foolish but she only really slept well with Aloysius sleeping in the same room. As far as the book went, her mother had loved it. It made Devon feel better whenever she was sad, to sit and read it.

However, what was all that about always being his sister? Maybe he was feeling more nervous than he let on.

She'd remember that exchange for a long time to come, and would even become haunted by his words. However, that wasn't going to happen today.

For now, Devon walked on with Melissa to sit outside the courtroom. They wouldn't let her inside for the arraignment. Once that was finished, there would be all kinds of discussions.

Things would move quickly and Devon hoped she could have one last conversation with Lucas. They had always been close and had told each other things.

The murders didn't make any sense to her. She wanted one last chance to try to make sense of it all. Devon also wanted that chance to ask Lucas why he did it.

....

I worked quickly, removing the belt from the new pants that they bought for me and wrapping it around the beam in the ceiling.

The place didn't have much, just a bed and a chair and table, not that I needed much but it was in the old part of the jail and so they still favored the higher ceilings. There was a hanger thing that looked strong enough. I looped one end of the belt around the hanger, making a larger loop big enough for my head to fit through. It was a good thing that there weren't any security cameras in here. I didn't want to be rescued. Not that it mattered much, not anymore.

I couldn't stand to see the wounded look in my sister's eyes, to know that I had been responsible for putting it there, even if I never intended for this to happen. Honest, I didn't.

All I wanted were answers and you'd think that would have solved everything, but if my father had known, he sure didn't share with me. He

74

claimed not to know. What was that all about?
Yeah, ask me if I believed him.

*He **had** to know, he just didn't want to tell me.*
Maybe Dad was protecting Mom but he died
without giving me the answers I had demanded.

As for Mom, well, she wasn't a whole lot better,
telling me that I didn't understand, but then not
even bothering to try and explain. Or maybe she
would have had I given her the chance.

I was just so furious when she told me I didn't
understand and then the gun went off and she
was lying there, bleeding to death. I was left
with even more questions than before.

Like, did Dad really not know? Was that even
possible? What happens next?

I know that a lot of people are going to call me a
coward, maybe even Devon will think that, but I
can't live the rest of my life behind bars. I can't.
Alice can work as hard as she wants to for that
insanity plea but it's never going to happen.
Either I'm going to jail, for life or I might get the
death penalty. Either way, I'm screwed.

Maybe someday, somehow, Devon will find out
the answers and maybe then she'll be able to
understand a little, to accept that it just had to
be this way. I laid everything out, the files, the
reports, all of it. All she has to do is find where I
hid everything.

75

I moved the chair, climbed up and stuck my head through the noose, tightening it around my neck. Taking a deep breath, I jumped, falling into darkness.

Chapter Eleven

It wasn't a private plane that Harrison used. He had access to the company jet. There were times, however, when first class was preferable. Here at least he could sit in relative privacy, enjoy a good meal, and some music. He could even watch a movie if the flight lasted long enough. The most important part was that he would be left to his own thoughts.

Both Greg and Susannah were dead, murdered by their only son, his only grandson. Lucas had found out. That was the only possible explanation. It was strange that instead of contacting his grandfather, Lucas had murdered his parents.

Everyone came to Harrison when they had problems. It was how his world worked. What had gone so wrong that Lucas didn't come to him? It simply made no sense. If he admired nothing else about the two of them, at least Harrison couldn't fault Greg and Susanna's parenting skills.

Lucas had grown into a sturdy, well-mannered, intelligent young man. He was good looking, sociable and had an entire life ahead of him.

His granddaughter, Devon was also turning out to be a young woman with a promising future. Well, he would arrange the double funeral and handle whatever else needed to be done. It was the least he could do.

It occurred to Harrison that Brad and Sylvie were most likely on their way as well, and a quick text message confirmed that.

It would take his surviving son and daughter-in-law more than three times the amount of travel time. That would put Harrison in full control; a position that he never questioned.

While flying to Erie, he spent his time productively, learning who the lawyer in charge was. Harrison was perplexed by the fact that so far no arraignment had taken place. It was past noon eastern time and even in such a small town, the wheels of justice should move more swiftly.

He did some googling, came up with a contact he knew that worked inside the courthouse and texted her, only to discover that there were rumors of something very wrong having just gone down. The woman assured Harrison that she would get back to him as soon as she learned more.

According to his watch, there were only ten minutes before the pilot would announce the need to turn off all electronic devices. He would have to wait. However, Harrison was a most patient man. It was what always worked for him. He had the ability to wait out his competition and it still served him well, especially when it came to personal matters. It was no surprise, therefore, that he was the secret keeper of this family.

Harrison just hoped that not too much of this particular rumor had been exposed prior to the murders. He felt competent enough to handle Lucas once he got there, to put a stop to anything that would take this too far.

On another airline, in business class, Brad and Sylvie sat silently. Their accommodations, though good enough to let Brad stretch his legs, were nowhere near the comfort of his father. Moreover, they had two transfers to look forward to with only enough time in Minnesota to grab a quick meal and use a full service restroom.

By the time Brad and Sylvie would get into town, they'd only be able to take a taxi to the hotel and leave word with Melissa that they had made it. They'd have enough time to catch some much needed sleep before the ten a.m. meeting tomorrow.

For herself, Sylvie was still struggling to understand just why Lucas had killed his parents.

They had last seen their nephew two months ago at his high school graduation party. It had been a normal and happy event as far as they could tell. Greg was beyond pleased about his son having been accepted into MIT.

Now, they were once more taking a long plane ride but this time, they would be arriving not as just the aunt and uncle, but as the legal guardians to their beloved niece.

What Devon must be going through, Sylvie could only imagine. The girl adored her big brother.

Now, she was alone, being tended to by strangers and having no idea how very much all their lives were about to change. Sylvie had a sudden, disturbing thought as she turned towards Brad.

"What if Devon doesn't want to live in Montana?"

"What?" Brad sounded distracted as he looked up from his phone. She should have known that he'd take advantage of having someone else handle the flying, in order for him to conduct business.

Sylvie tried again, this time placing her hand on his shoulder and squeezing gently for emphasis.

"Devon may not want to move back with us."

It was a concern that had plagued her almost as soon as they were settled in their seats. After all, the girl had a life there in Erie, with friends and everything that she was used to. With Lucas having killed their parents, it meant that Devon would have to leave everything and everyone she had ever known. Sylvie wasn't so sure that the girl would go willingly.

"Of course she'll come with us. It's not like she has a choice, Sylvie." Brad tried to be patient as he explained the situation as he saw it. "We live in Montana. As her legal guardians, that's where she's going to live until she turns eighteen."

Sylvie just shook her head. Men could be so dense.

It wasn't as if Devon was stubborn or uncooperative, but they might have to come up with some sort of compromise unless they wanted the girl to spend even more time with a therapist.

Her own phone beeped and she glanced down to read a quick text from Glenda. After reading it, she sighed, and then waved the post in front of her husband's eyes so that he could read it through. The double murder had hit the net and was not only being covered by Erie's local paper; *Erie Times News*, but had hit most of the other top news media as well.

At least there weren't any pictures of Devon because she was still a minor. Greg, Susanna, and Lucas all received full pictures. Most of the details were being kept to a minimum, most likely due to her father-in-law's considerable influence. Still, there were details that had managed to be leaked to the press. There were always people willing to talk; you had to be crafty enough to find them.

Sylvie was quite sure that by the time they would be eating breakfast tomorrow Harrison would have the entire situation handled.

To be fair, he only had to travel from Chicago, giving him a full day's head start. Still, she knew how much he adored his grandchildren. They were lucky to have him heading up the family, Sylvie thought as she laid her head back against the cushioned headrest, closing her eyes.

Chapter Twelve

Alice had only just started to talk with Melissa. She wanted to discuss how she saw this particular case progressing. Suddenly, there were shouts for medical personnel, which had her at a half run. Alice was hampered by wearing four-inch heels, but she ran as fast as she could, even as she felt her breath hitching. Oh shit, no, it couldn't... He was fine, just a kid and there were no signs...

Still, she felt her heart hammering as she reached the holding cell area. Alice noted with despair, mingled with self-reproach, that the medics had already arrived.

They were loading a body onto a stretcher and were telling the bystanders to get out of their way. She had to look of course, had to see for herself the motionless slumped figure that a mere half hour ago, had been that of her client, Lucas Fielding. Now, he too was dead.

Alice got that much just by raising her eyebrows at the man nearest her and with a slow shake of his head, knew that there was no chance left for a quick miracle.

The CSI team was already in the holding cell, going over all of the evidence, as she peered around the corner. Alice took a good, long look, knowing that she could go no further inside, at least not yet. There was a broken belt lying on the floor, clearly that had been what he had used.

A hanging suicide after two murders meant that she would have the unfortunate task of informing the rest of his family.

Oh major shit, shit, shit, she thought. Harrison Fielding was on his way here. He would demand not just answers but her head, if she remembered anything else about him. His beloved grandson, and there had not been even a mention of placing the boy on a suicide watch.

If there was hell to pay, it would be on Alice to pay it, unless she managed to do some very quick juggling of her own.

Alice yanked out her phone, ignoring the legion of texts that waited for her and sent a text to Price, who answered almost immediately. Yes, he knew about the suicide, he had just been notified, but he was already talking to the two detectives in charge of the case.

So far, not one person considered Lucas to be a suicide risk and he was working on them to make sure he got that in writing.

Great minds think alike she posted back, pleased and a little relieved as she took her phone and headed down to her supervisor's office, to explain face to face.

Alice took a deep breath before walking inside and shutting the door behind her as directed. She walked over to the desk where her supervisor sat.

He was an older man, somewhere in his mid fifties, with black hair ruthlessly buzz cut against his scalp, his eyes were like black ice, as they stared at her for a very long minute. Then, he motioned for her to sit. He leaned back in his chair, locking the fingers of both hands together, before he spoke.

Alice had kept quiet the entire time. She knew from painful experience that it would serve her much better to let him do the talking and to answer his questions. It was not a good idea to volunteer any information.

Funny, but those were the same instructions that she had given to Lucas, the same ones she gave to every one of her clients. Alice knew that depending on how well she conducted herself, and how thorough her answers to whatever he asked, she would either have to start looking for another job almost immediately or else she would have him on her side when she went up against Harrison.

She rather hoped for the latter, but time would tell as her supervisor started shooting rapid-fire questions at her.

"How is it that there was no suicide watch on this young man? Did the sister know anything about this crime before it happened? Did your client tell the sister anything that will be a problem now that he's dead? What about the detectives? Do they agree that there was no need for a watch?"

Alice explained that at no time during her meetings with Lucas did he exhibit any behaviors that indicated he was even briefly contemplating suicide. She also told him that the detectives agreed with her assessment. No, the sister knew nothing about her brother's plans prior to the incident, and she had learned nothing from him while they had met at the jail.

The rest of the questions were just as rapid fire and she thought that she had satisfied him.

Sometimes with Sam Burrows, there just was no telling until he either let you hang or let you off the hook. Today, the gods were ruling in her favor as he nodded.

"Alright, Carrins, you've convinced me. I want to be informed the second you make contact with Harrison Fielding and let me remind you in case you don't already know.

The man is connected with various news sources as well as high priced lawyers. He can still break you and end your career if he is of a mind to. This office has your back, but you need to respond to him the way you have here. Close the door on your way out."

Alice nodded and got to her feet, leaving as quietly as she had entered and smiled with a single thumb up when several heads lifted from their terminals as she walked back down the hall.

She had a good reputation and it was well deserved, but that didn't mean that she could just coast on that rep either. Until she got things squared away with the powerful grandfather, she was still going to feel jumpy and ill at ease. She wasn't going to show it though, that would make the difference.

"Alice, you got a sec?" It was Doug Pritchard, primary crime scene responder. Because of his expertise regarding firearms, he was the one called to the initial shooting scene at the Fielding house. Doug had collected both guns and was still processing them. "Sure, what can I do for you?"

Doug came over to where she was standing and lowered his voice. "It's about that suicide we're investigating. I know we found the belt around the kid's neck but that's not how he died."

What? Alice frowned, thinking that maybe she had bought herself some time here. "What are you saying, Doug?" She kept her voice low too, and stepped closer to him.

"I'm saying that the kid hit his head when he landed.
The doctors at the hospital are calling it a suicide and I know that he intended to kill himself.

That's not how he died though. The belt broke before that happened. At his height and adding in the height of that beam from the floor below, it doesn't add up. The belt wasn't strong enough to hold him up. When it broke, that's when the kid fell. It's looking like he was still alive when he landed."

Alice shook her head. "What are the chances that you can prove exactly how he died?"

Doug just shrugged his shoulders. "It's too early to tell, but we might get lucky. I'll say this much though. The doctors are the ones to call it and I think they're going to call it a suicide. I don't know if this helps you out at all, but I figured you'd want to know."

"I do and thanks for your help, Doug. Please keep me updated." "Yeah, I'll do that, Alice."

He nodded again and headed back down to the lab.

Chapter Thirteen

Harrison Fielding was a presence in his own right even while he played the worried grandfather role. He stormed into Melissa Daniels office without even knocking. As soon as she saw him, Devon jumped out of her chair and practically flew into his outstretched arms, and was held tight.

"How's my darling girl? Are they treating you like the princess you are?" A hard stare out of green eyes was directed towards Melissa who shot an equally hard stare back at him. He might be the head of the Fielding family, but she was no pushover. Her voice, when she spoke was firm.

"Devon has been in my constant care, Mr. Matthews. You can be assured of that."

He held his granddaughter for a few more minutes. Harrison then held Devon at arms' length, studying the flushed face, the eyes that showed ravages of past crying. His hand was gentle as it stroked slowly down her cheek. He turned his attention on Melissa at that point, his hand now on Devon's shoulder, maintaining that contact.

"Devon is my only granddaughter and very precious to me. "

He turned back to the young girl, guiding her more comfortably into a thickly cushioned chair.

"Brad and Sylvie will be here tomorrow and we can talk then about what comes next, Devon. Do you want anything to eat? I've heard that there are some excellent restaurants nearby, more than ready to provide take out. You can have anything you want."

Devon shook her head though, since she kept feeling half-nauseous and more than a little scared. Food, even the thought of it, wasn't helping her much.

"I'm Ok, Grandpa, really. I guess I'll spend tonight with Melissa and then we'll all talk tomorrow."

Harrison knew how the system worked and he wasn't about to make waves with Protective Services. He was more than willing to be cooperative.

"That sounds like a plan, darling. I have a hotel room close by. I just want to talk to Lucas' public defender, get the details on the case, and then get some lunch. You should eat even if it's just a few bites and then lie down a while. You need rest and some food."

Harrison passed a hand over her hair as he spoke to her and for a minute she leaned against his shoulder, feeling comforted.

Devon always felt safe with her grandfather. He was the man who handled things and kept secrets, no matter how small or unimportant they might be.

He never laughed at her or made her revelations seem insignificant, and it only increased their bond with one another.

Devon could tell her grandfather anything and had often shared her confidences with him. She even texted him for advice now and then.

She knew that even though he called her princess, he let her make her own decisions, and made it clear that he thought her bright and capable. He never saw her as a helpless female child. Devon never felt inadequate, not with him, not ever.

Alice had stood there, watching the entire scene in silence, her expression difficult to read. Harrison Fielding appeared to be cooperative, but she sensed that there was something else beneath the surface. She reminded herself to remain cautious in her dealings with him.

With his granddaughter and Melissa both in the same room, it was easy enough to play to the crowd, so to speak.

Alice would have to remain on her guard, make sure that whatever control she thought herself to possess, stayed as it was.

Harrison turned his attention towards Alice as she finished her thought and just then, his phone beeped. His reaction as he read the text was lightning fast. She almost thought she had imagined that the friendly green eyes had turned to frozen shards of anger.

Alice tried to convince herself that she had only imagined the look because before she could look over at Harrison once more, he had himself well under control, his hand soothing as he stroked his granddaughter's hair one more time before rising easily from his chair.

"Let me talk privately to Miss Carrins, darling and I'll be back."

"Devon will be just fine with me, Mr. Fielding.," Melissa's tone was reassuring even as her eyes briefly met Alice's, a quick message in them to watch her step which Alice acknowledged with a quick little nod of her head.

"If you'll come this way, Mr. Fielding, I'll find us a nice, quiet room where we can talk."

Alice led the way without even pausing to check on whether he was following her. Harrison found that amusing as he walked behind her, his large frame dwarfing her more delicate build. Alice navigated the twists and turns of the hallway with her usual brisk walk, finding an unused interrogation room and opening it to allow him to enter first. Once he was seated, she took the chair opposite him, studying him cautiously.

"I take it that the text in question had to do with Lucas's suicide."

There, she'd said it outright, so that they could deal with the elephant in the room as she sat there, her spine ramrod stiff, not permitting her back to touch any part of the chair she sat on. Harrison on the other hand, leaned comfortably back in his own seat, and kept his green eyes on hers.

What Harrison saw in front of him was a delicately built young woman with the poise and confidence of a woman decades older. It almost amused him how she had taken control of the situation and led him here in the first place.

"Yes. Am I to believe that you want to discuss just how we tell my granddaughter? It's the only likely explanation for why she didn't know. According to my text, my grandson has been lying in the city morgue for well over two hours."

He was a tall and powerfully built man, one who obviously worked out, kept in top shape and one who commanded a sizable empire. It was like watching a lion out of his den and Alice intended to handle him carefully.

"We have several excellent grief therapists on the city payroll, Mr. Fielding. I can in fact have the best of that group here within the hour. It might be best if we defer to his professional opinion instead of making things even more difficult for Devon."

He made a sniffing sound at that.

"I don't know how we can make things any more difficult for a young woman, who has now lost her entire immediate family, Ms. Carrins, but go ahead, make your phone call." He paused, having never taken his eyes off her.

"I have all the time in the world."

Why that particular way of phrasing things irritated her, Alice couldn't say, but she nodded her head and pulled out her phone. Finding the name she needed, she sent an urgent series of text messages, outlining the situation and letting Robert Paul know that he was needed as soon as reasonably possible.

The returning texts reassured her that Robert had nothing more pressing on his schedule now and promised her that he would be there shortly.

She looked up from her phone to find that she was still being watched.

"You're John and Lucinda's daughter. You're also known as the woman that the courts refer to as the terrier of the public defender's office." Harrison's tone was matter of fact as he continued to stare at her.

"That's right. You're familiar with them?"

It was possible of course since her parents were great patrons of the arts and Harrison himself had been known to give and quite generously to a number of philanthropic enterprises.

He waved his hand a little.

"We've met on several occasions. Tell me, Ms. Carrins, was there any reason why you elected not to put my grandson on a suicide watch?"

Ah, there it was the question of the hour, and the one she was the most prepared to answer.

"Lucas simply never showed any indications that he was depressed or suicidal. His responses were in full, complete sentences. He was easy to understand, he certainly wasn't overly emotional, nor was he detached from the situation. In fact, he had spent over an hour being grilled by our two top criminal detectives and both concur with my opinion."

"I'm sure that they did and it's interesting that you took the time to find that out, Ms. Carrins. Were you perhaps warned that I might not take it too well to discover that he had been left alone for at least a half an hour with a means to that end?" He paused to let that sink in for a few minutes. "My grandson was a boy scout for a few years when he was younger. He could quite easily survive a night or two in the wilderness alone so I'm quite sure he could also figure out how to hang himself."

Well, that was calling a spade a spade, wasn't it? Apparently, Alice had shown some of her inner turmoil because he continued, his own expression turning ruthless.

"Shocked you, didn't it? I don't waste time, Ms. Carrins and I want a few answers from you, before we let this grief counselor have his own say on the matter."

"Of course, what do you want to know? I should warn you that I too don't like to waste time, so if any of your questions end up just being a repeat of asking why Lucas was left alone, I'd personally advise you to skip them and move on."

Another amused smile, this time directed towards her and it made her see if for only the briefest of moments, how people could come to trust, even to like this man. At least, they could when he made the effort to be just a little charming.

"Fill me in on what he told you and yes." Harrison held up a hand as she started to protest.

"I know you can't reveal what was said in confidence between client and lawyer. However, indulge me a little. My grandson is dead, surely that confidentiality doesn't apply here and if it does, what harm could possibly be done if you let me know this much. Did he tell you why he did it?"

Harrison was right that Lucas was dead but as for the rest of what he said? Alice simply shook her head.

"I have to disagree with you, Mr. Fielding. According to the U.S. Supreme Court case of Swidler & Berlin v. United States, the Court ruled that the attorney-client privilege survived the man's death. If Lucas had an estate where we needed to gain clarification of his testamentary intentions, then that would be a different story altogether. I can understand your frustrations but it's my duty to uphold the law. Therefore, I can't reveal any of my client's confidential statements to me." She paused. "I'm sure you understand."

Harrison Fielding wouldn't be the first family member to try and gather any information he could that wasn't actually his to learn.

"I can tell you this much. He never explained to me why he killed his parents and he never tried to explain any of it to Devon either. Your guess is as good as mine."

Guess. Hmmm, well that would be the word he'd used if he were in her shoes but Harrison didn't need to guess. He had a good idea of just why Lucas did it since it all pointed right back to that secret. He must have found out and for some reason or other, didn't get the answers he most wanted. Harrison sincerely doubted that the boy had intent, but the results were still the same.

The fact that he had killed himself told his grandfather that the boy had felt remorse, and was aware that his own life would be over and for a very long time. The Fielding men in general, if one was not killed off, tended to live well into their nineties. That meant a very long time behind bars indeed for Lucas had he not succeeded in his suicide attempt.

The knock on the door had both sets of eyes turning as it opened to admit a nondescript man in his mid thirties dressed casually in a sports coat and corduroy pants. He wore a pair of wire-rimmed glasses and managed to look both competent and approachable.

"Alice? I got here as quickly as I could. I was just finishing up dictating my notes from my last appointment and I stopped by your office in order to get some basic background on your client."

He turned towards Harrison next, sizing up the man quickly and coming to the same conclusions that Alice had. This man of power didn't suffer fools gladly. Robert was not a fool. He was one of the best at his job, but even he felt a little out of place, hoping that it wouldn't be obvious.

"Robert Paul, Mr. Fielding. You have my sincere sympathy on your loss." His hand was out right away towards Harrison who took in the man's appearance and general potential in minutes. At least the grip was firm and Robert easily met his eyes. That said a lot to him.

"Thank you."

Before Harrison could add to that statement, Alice had taken over, again.

"We want to be sure that this matter be handled as gently as possible, Robert, since Devon hasn't been told yet about her brother's suicide."

Robert frowned a little.

"That's going to make things more difficult but perhaps if the three of us were there together, that might help." He turned back to Harrison.

"It might be a good idea for you to present the news to your granddaughter, Mr. Fielding. That way, coming from a member of her own family, well, it would make my job that much easier and I could start to work with her right away with you providing what comfort you can."

"Of course, be glad to do it."

Chapter Fourteen

"Why? Why would he do that? "She was sobbing almost hysterically, clutching at her grandfather as if he was her only lifeline. He was the only member of her family who was with her now.

"We don't know why, darling, we probably never will. This nice young man, Robert, is going to work with you, help you through this. Don't worry, I won't leave you. I'll just sit over there in the corner. You'll know I'm there but I won't get in the way."

Not as long as I do my job, you won't, Robert thought to himself.

IIe knew enough about Harrison Fielding to know that they all had to be on their best game. Well, he was as up to the challenge as anyone could be.

Robert quickly took over, starting to work with Devon. It didn't take long before both appeared to almost forget that there was that third party in the room.

Meanwhile, down the hall, Melissa and Alice were having a cup of coffee and splitting a bag of animal crackers from the vending machine.

"Let's hope the guardians get here early enough tomorrow. I keep getting the feeling that they're the only reason the lion hasn't scooped up his granddaughter and carried her away to safety somewhere."

Alice chuckled a little.

"He does cut quite a commanding presence, doesn't he? According to him, the other son and daughter-in-law should make it in late tonight. I'm expecting to meet with them in my office tomorrow around ten. That gives all of us time to sleep and then have some breakfast. I'm lucky that Mr. Fielding allowed enough time in the schedule." She shrugged her shoulders. "He's trying not to order me around which you know I won't stand for, no matter how powerfully connected the man is." Alice sipped her coffee.

"All I can say is I'm glad that I don't have to spend a lot of time around him. You have to admire a guy who's that devoted to his family. I know that I still have to meet her future guardians, but I think that Devon's going to be alright. She has strong family support and it's only for two years. Once she turns eighteen, she can make her own choices, legally. I've worked wonders with less." Melissa occasionally glanced down at her phone and the texts that continued to come in regarding this case while she talked.

Alice glanced down at her own phone, noting the time, and then sent off a few quick texts as well before getting back to her feet and tossing out the empty coffee cup and napkin.

"I'll take your word on that, Melissa. The first session with Rob is about over so I want to see what else we can do for Devon before releasing her back into your custody until tomorrow."

Melissa was already standing by the door, having cleaned up her own things.

"Maybe there's something she really wants or needs from her house. I know she can't go in there yet but having a few of her things can really help her at a time like this."

"Sure, good idea. I'll ask her about it. Let's get going. I don't want to give Mr. Fielding even the slightest opening to preach on how I'm not doing my job."

"He has to know that you have other cases though." Melissa had other clients as well that needed some checks, but in this situation, Devon was getting the majority of her time and attention.

"I don't think it crosses his mind that I have anything else on my plate but taking care of his granddaughter."

The door was open by the time they had come back, with Rob shaking hands with both Devon and her grandfather and it looked like everything had gone well. To her unspoken question, he smiled a little at her.

"It was a good first session, Alice. I think we made some headway, but she's going to need some down time to process this and I promised to be in touch.

I understand that her guardians will be here tomorrow so I've made an appointment to meet with her and them before they leave town."

"That's a good idea, Rob, thanks. I'll take it from here."

She looked over at Devon who was talking softly to her grandfather. Whatever it was that she had said, it made the older man laugh a little as he stroked her hair, nodding his agreement. Looking up, his green eyes focused directly on Alice as he rose easily from his seat, to stride over to her and Melissa.

"My granddaughter has a list of items she wants from her room." He handed over the piece of paper.

"I assured her that it wouldn't be any trouble to handle her request." It wasn't so much a question, but a statement of fact. Alice took the paper and scanned down the few items written there.

"I'll have these personally delivered back to where she's staying." She paused, knowing it was best to maintain eye contact as much as possible.

"Is there anything else I can do for you? If not, I have other duties that need my attention and

Melissa is going to be with Devon until your son and daughter-in-law arrive."

Harrison nodded a little. Smart and capable woman, he thought, but he kept that to himself.

"I'm going back to my hotel, get some of my own work done, but I'll be here for the meeting with Brad and Sylvie tomorrow." He stopped at the door, turning around with his hand on the doorknob.

"I want to thank you for how well you've treated my granddaughter, Ms. Carrins. She's a bright and capable young woman who's been dealt a very nasty life altering series of changes. Once she receives the items on her list and sees her aunt and uncle again, she'll start moving in the right direction to heal."

He would personally see to it even though he believed that Sylvie and Brad would do well by their niece.

"I'm the best in my job, Mr. Fielding even if that doesn't usually lend itself to the care of the client's family, though I've made an exception in this case."

She let him go first down the hall and then she followed, turning right while he went left and making her way back to her office. Alice was soon immersed in answering calls and processing paperwork. The light was fading by the time she had finished wading through the worst of it, and she noted with some relief that it was only a little after six in the evening. She decided to call it a night, have some dinner and an early bedtime.

Chapter Fifteen

Looks like everyone's getting ready to move to that next part of their lives, doesn't it? I mean, geez, I only just killed two people and then myself in what? Twenty four hours? But life moves on, at least for the living which I'm not and yeah, to say it sucks, is a major understatement. But this is still my story and I still have a say in it even if no one else is focusing on me.

Well, tomorrow my aunt and uncle will get here and yeah, there will be all kinds of meetings and boring talks and at the end, three funerals before Devon heads back with them and we all start over.

Of course I'm not sure about the whole suicide thing and how that's going to work for a funeral, but you've met my grandfather, right? He's the guy with connections and the persistence to see things through. Harrison Fielding gets what he wants, first, last and always. It's always been that way, but he's never been a pain about it. You know?

I mean, I probably could have gone to him when I first found out about all of this. He would have helped. I know that he would have. Shocked, stunned, angry, whatever, he still would have helped. So, why didn't I go to him when I found out? I don't know. I only know part of this secret thing so maybe that's why. Course he could have helped me get all the rest of my answers. Then, I wouldn't have had to handle things the way that I did.

But what eighteen year old really thinks this stuff out? I didn't have a lot of time to think about any of it before I just reacted. That's the worst part. I reacted and look what happened to what's left of my family. I made some pretty bad decisions and now it's too late to change any of it.

I'm not even here, not really. Well, kinda since I'm drifting around, listening, that sort of thing. I can't explain it and I can't control where I go now. I'm just around, if you know what I mean. You probably don't and that's cool. They're all talking about me though and that helps, a little. I mean, I loved these people and they loved me. No one is badmouthing me either; they're just trying to understand what went wrong.

I can't explain it myself, so good luck to any of them in coming up with answers that they can live with. That's what's going to be the end of things.

They'll finally come up with answers that they can live with so that they can move on. Funny thing is that I'd do it that way too.

....

Back to the present, again...

The hotel was a decent one for being so close to the courthouse and not that expensive.

107

Harrison always stayed at the best that the city could provide.

This particular hotel though was middle of the road if he had to judge it. The car and driver were first rate as they delivered him right to the door. The bellhop helped him with his bags and within twenty minutes, he was inside his room, checking out the small map and changing into work out clothes. He badly needed to work out the stress of this difficult day.

First, his son and daughter-in-law were murdered and now his grandson commits suicide instead of facing what he did and for what? A secret like that should have never seen the light of day. Now, he would never know what if anything, Greg had known.

What was most puzzling was the fact that Lucas never came to him for help. Harrison thought that they had a tight bond, not just, because he was the boy's grandfather but because they had spent a lot of time together over the years. However, at this most confusing and upsetting time in his life, Lucas never once reached out to him. That was the most frustrating part of all of this.

Everyone called on Harrison. That's how it worked in his world and he thrived on that, on helping people find their way out of their messes, personal as well as professional. Not Lucas though.

The boy decided to handle this on his own and look what happened as a result. Three dead people, their names, and faces splashed all over the media, including the complimentary local paper sitting on the front desk at check in.

The female clerk was young and obviously recognized Harrison as she kept her face averted from his. She managed to handle the registration calmly and efficiently, with not one trace of emotion on her face. The girl was good at her job, but it was disconcerting to find himself in such a situation. Yes, he really did need that gym.

Pocketing his key and carrying a change of clothes in his bag, he made his way down the stairs to the lower level gym. He stowed his gear in the combination locker provided, then took a quick inventory of what was here.

They didn't have a bench press, but they had mats and several sets of dumbbells along with some very up to date machines, including several treadmills. Not bad, not bad at all, he thought, as he did his warm up stretches first. Once he was limber enough to move on, Harrison set up the weights and moved into position. Using the wide grip the way he had been trained, he did three sets of ten repetitions. The decline dumbbell press and another three sets of ten repetitions each followed these.

Once he was finished with his repetitions, he easily moved over to the incline press that looked brand new. That suited Harrison just fine as he did his three sets of ten repetitions. He then completed the chest and triceps portion of his workout with overhead extensions using the set of dumbbells for another three sets.

He was glad to see that at this time of day, no one else was in here, as he wanted to be alone. If others were around, he would have adapted otherwise and used his set of earphones to drown out the hard rock usually being blasted in the background.

There wasn't a need for that now, thankfully, as Harrison moved through the rest of his workout. He went to work on his back and biceps by using the Olympic bar curls with a split stance, before moving right along to work on his shoulders and abdominal muscles.

Harrison was seriously ripped for a man of his age. Hell, for a man of any age, he was seriously ripped and he took his exercising seriously. He rarely missed the opportunity to work every part of his body. Harrison liked mixing up the order somewhat, but still covering every part.

The dumbbells provided here were good quality and the mat where he was lying had been freshly cleaned. It made it easier to do his crunches, sit-ups and leg raises, not to mention the oblique crunches.

Harrison smoothly moved from the mat to the various machines, adjusting the weights as needed. He occasionally mopped his face with the rented towel as he exercised.

Remembering that today was Thursday, he walked over to the nearest treadmill, programming in a medium run of three miles at a brisk pace.

This helped to clear his mind and allowed him to focus on what he could control now, and that was this workout.

He had a personal trainer back home in Chicago, and Jack had been excellent in programming a traveling exercise routine, that would fit in wherever Harrison found himself.

There were many times when he would be reduced to using just his body weight and an exercise band, having to run outside in semi-darkness or even up and down stairs when nothing else was available. Harrison was fortunate to be in a place so well equipped and he saw no reason to deny himself.

There was even a hot tub where he went at the end of his workout, allowing the hot water to soak out whatever tension might still be lingering. He was careful to set the timer, so that he wouldn't overdo.

It would be very easy to let that happen and he wasn't about to add to the personal trauma of his family. By this time tomorrow, the funerals would be scheduled. Devon would be reunited with her aunt and uncle, and the rest of the details would be settled. With luck, Harrison would be home in Chicago by the beginning of next week.

Chapter Sixteen

"Why should you be surprised to find that we're all booked in the same hotel?"

Sylvie sat on the bed in their hotel room suite, sipping an excellent cup of coffee as she absently watched her husband dress. "I'm not. Ok, I guess I shouldn't be but I am."

Brad finished dressing, waiting now for his wife to finish her coffee and slide her feet into a pair of brown heels. They matched the rather somber dress she'd chosen for today and the series of meetings.

Sylvie wanted to appear calm, orderly, and confident for her niece. She very much wanted to be an oasis for Devon so that she'd feel safe and protected, much the way that Harrison had wanted things. She herself had had no conversation with her father-in-law on this, or on any other family matters. In fact, Sylvie rarely spoke to Harrison, seeing the man only a handful of times a year.

It wasn't quite the close-knit family she'd hoped for when she and Brad had married, but every time Sylvie brought up the subject or came anywhere close to discussing it, she found the proverbial closed door.

There were reasons why Brad had left Erie and moved to Montana, leaving the main headquarters of the thriving family business as well as his only brother and sister-in-law.

It wasn't because they couldn't stand each other. The Fieldings got together every year for Thanksgiving, Christmas, and Easter and they all appeared to get along well.

Sylvie couldn't find any tension in any of them, which meant that either they were all superb actors or that they did indeed get along. For some reason that she didn't understand though, they remained scattered from one another, only communicating for holidays or major events.

Her family was too small to really count. Being born to two only children meant that there were no aunts and uncles, no cousins and only the faintest of memories of grandparents.

In fact, her father died in a plane crash, leaving her at the age of ten. Her mother died, four months after her marriage to Brad. Her stepfather had passed away six months later. Sylvie soon realized that the Fieldings were now her family. Since they were the only family she had, Sylvie kept pushing Brad to move closer to his brother and family. However, he refused to do so, appearing content to visit only a few times a year.

Brad was a gifted photographer who could easily have made a successful living at it, but he considered it as more of a hobby. Sylvie herself was an interior designer who could live and work anywhere, but Brad insisted on staying in Montana. He still worked at the family business but only at one of the smaller plants.

Maybe with taking Devon to live with them, things might change, but she doubted it.

Her husband was very much rooted in his ways. Besides, it was probably better that Devon left Pennsylvania and started a new life far away from all of the bad memories.

Brad for his part was doing his best to school his features before they got to the meeting this morning. He knew that his father would be present as he was in every other event in this family. Brad also knew that Sylvie would take this as an opportunity to step up her campaign for them to move back here, and even with Susanna and Greg's deaths, that wasn't an option in his book. Brad had his own reasons for leaving town right after his brother's wedding, but he couldn't possibly share any of them with his wife.

How would it look to try and explain that he was still in love with the girl that was now and forevermore his sister-in-law? Susanna had chosen Greg, was pregnant at the time of the marriage so how could she possibly change her mind?

Susanna was well aware that by marrying while being pregnant, there would be talk. Even if they tried to move the wedding up by one month, there would be those people who would be counting on their fingers. There would also be those who would accept the explanation of the first-born baby being a larger than normal child, or so Susanna thought.

Brad half snorted to himself as he and Sylvie took the elevator down to the parking garage. No one really believed that now, did they?

However, even if they pretended to accept the lie, no one knew that Brad was in love with his own brother's wife.

Sure, he had done his part as the best man, orchestrating a wild bachelor party, complete with strippers and a girl jumping out of the cake. Brad had also managed to deliver a wedding day toast that sounded heartfelt, even though he was sure that all the guests there could hear the pounding of his heart, while he looked at Greg and Susanna up there on the dais.

He had held up his glass of pink champagne, inviting the guests to join in on the toast, and had marveled at the fact that the pink tint in the bride's water glass had the same coloring as the champagne; it was even sparkling water, another nice touch.

There had been the one moment of panic when Greg had tapped him on the shoulder while he was dancing with the maid of honor before handing Susanna over. Greg had made a joking warning about his not trying to steal the bride. The maid of honor had laughed and then Brad found himself holding Susanna again.

The silence between them grew awkward until she whispered that people would start to talk if they didn't fake it a little. Therefore, he put on his social face and looked down at her.

"Why, Susanna? Why did you choose Greg? You know how I feel about you."

"Shhh, and lower your voice, would you. I don't want to be overheard. Think of the scandal that would cause."

"Scandal? You think being pregnant and then getting married isn't enough of a scandal?"

She glared up at him and then fought back the look, forcing her lips to curl into something half way resembling a smile.

"Don't start that again, Brad. You know why I married Greg. I'm pregnant, remember? If I changed my mind and married the other brother, all of our lives as we know them, would be over and no, I'm not being overly dramatic and you know it.

Greg is the right choice and I intend to do my very best to make sure he never regrets this. Besides, we both want to start a family; we're just starting earlier than most."

"You're not even out of college yet and with a baby on the way, how do you plan on finishing your classes?"

Susanna tossed her head in simple defiance, a move he was well accustomed to, which strangely enough, he still found arousing.

"The baby is due in August, and my last class is in May. I may waddle down the aisle to pick up my diploma but at least I'll have a wedding ring on my finger. I'll even be a Fielding instead of a Gold the way I had originally planned it."

Ouch. He deserved that even as he winced.

"I tried to explain ..." He was cut off as she held up a hand briefly, still smiling that fake half smile of hers, the polite society one that she seemed able to put on and take off easily.

"I remember that too, Brad, or should I call you Fred? It's very confusing, even now, especially with these hormones from hell clouding my brain cells."

The music ended with a clapping of hands as she stepped out of his arms. Before she turned back towards her husband, Susanna sent Brad a pitying glance.

"When you find a girl willing to marry you, at least be sure you've given her your right name first. It helps a lot to start off with honesty in a relationship, which is why ours ended."

With that scathing retort, she departed. From that moment until the day she died, they had never discussed their meeting, nor had they spent too much time alone. Susanna saw to that, making sure that they were usually part of a group. She also easily deflected each and every attempt he had made over the years to change things. Finally, Brad gave in, accepting that as far as she was concerned, there had never been anyone else for her but Greg.

Chapter Seventeen
Several years in the past...

Alpha and Omega Fraternity House held a big, blowout party the second Saturday of September for as long as any of its alumni had "known. There were never any invitations to their three-storied Grecian style building, at least not for this gathering. For most of the attendees, it would be their only opportunity to get inside. It was usually the cream at the university lucky enough to pledge, let alone be accepted. They only took on twenty pledges a year and from that number selected at the very most, four.

Their hazing episodes were legendary and daring, even dangerous at times, and bordering on illegal. Thanks in large part to the influential and wealthy parentage of their illustrious alumni they always managed to stay just ahead of the law.

Susanna Travers had convinced two of her best friends to come along with her for the annual toga party. Each one of them was draped in an inexpensive version of the togas made famous by Animal House. They even went so far as to wear flowered wreaths on their heads. The girls were all freshmen and had been assured of a good time. Susanna knew that this might be their only chance to stir things up a little. If they were lucky, they might meet a gorgeous upperclassman, have a little flirt going and who knows what else. Julia Jacobsen, her best friend and roommate had talked nonstop about what drinks to accept. She reminded both girls about always knowing where their drinks were.

Susanna just nodded, letting her friend be the voice of reason for the evening while she and Frannie giggled excitedly at their luck in being at a frat party. Their eyes slowly adjusted to the dim lighting and their ears to the pounding rock music that poured out of the house and down the street. The fraternity's neighbors stayed inside,_shaking their heads and asking themselves why they ever thought it was a good idea to live so close to the most popular frat house in the area.

"Have a beer."

A tall guy with wild brown hair and a warm smile pressed a can into her slender hand.

"Welcome to A and O. My name is Fred. My major is engineering."

"Susanna. I'm an education major. It's nice to meet you, Fred. These are my friends, Julia and Frannie. "

"It's nice to meet you girls." He smiled at them, handing each a can of beer before grabbing Susanna's hand.

"Let's dance."

She pressed her unopened can of beer into Julia's ever-watchful hands and ended up dancing the rest of the night away with this very attentive guy.

He looked like a worthy specimen, tall, dark and somewhat cute, not to mention, older. He certainly didn't sound like or even look like a freshmen. As Julia was forever saying, Susanna could certainly pick her guys and she was right on all counts.

Fred was a senior, she learned later in the evening. Unlike most guys her age, he wasn't adverse to talking about himself and asking about her, like he was really interested. In addition, he certainly seemed smitten as her mother liked to say. He even asked for her phone number, insisting on walking the girls back to their dorm at close to midnight, ever mindful that they had curfews.

"Too bad about the midnight curfew thing, we could have had a really good time." Fred smiled though when he spoke. His smile put her at ease. She really liked this guy.

He didn't try for a kiss, not that Susanna would have refused him, though she'd see if he called like he said he would. Guys didn't always do that, even if you put out the first time, not that he tried to drag her into an unused bedroom. No, Fred behaved himself, talking to her, dancing and making sure she had a good time. Susanna had such a good time in fact that when

122

he called the next day to ask her out, she
accepted, right on the spot.

They went to the movies, to sporting events,
had dinners together, and took long, romantic
walks around Presque Isle in the late
afternoons after classes were over for the day.
Susanna couldn't help but fall for this great,
gorgeous guy. Fred was everything she had
ever wanted and she had dreamed big. She
figured that he had to come from money
because he never once complained about not
having enough.

Both of them would suggest activities, taking
turns and he never once told her that he
couldn't afford something. There was also the
spiffy Mustang that Fred drove, which was only
four years old. He said that the car was a high
school graduation gift from his father, though
he didn't talk that much about his family.

Everything was going well except for one small
detail. Well, not exactly small and she did let
Fred know as soon as they started dating so
that everything would be out in the open.

Greg, of course was the "one small detail." He
was a junior marketing major with dark hair
cut very short to his head, emphasizing his dark
brown eyes. He was a few inches taller than
her which meant that she could still wear heels.
Greg and Susanna had met the very first day of
her orientation and had been inseparable from
then on. They didn't go out a whole lot, just
occasional movies or study dates. Susanna

really liked him. Usually, she had been drawn to adventurous types or even the proverbial bad guy. One of his main attractions was that he was a Fielding, which meant that he came from a rich family. Greg was more down to earth though and he never flaunted his wealthy background.

This was the first time Susanna had dated two guys that were just great guys without any particular drama. She had to create her own, which she did simply by dating them both and then telling them about the other one.

Susanna conveniently left out the part of the guy's names so that they could never know who she was dating. Luckily, she never seemed to see Fred if she was out with Greg. The same happened when she was out with Greg.

Julia was appalled, telling her that she couldn't treat guys that way, and warning her roomie that she was going to be dumped by both of them. She had even predicted the dire results to include being shunned by all the other guys at the university, but strangely enough, that never happened.

Susanna ended up continuing to date both guys and was also pursued by numerous others, especially when there was a school event.

Julia and Frannie both thought that once they all graduated, that Susanna would have to finally make a choice; she would either have to pick one of the two guys or break up with them both and move on. A decision was looming and she would have to make her choice.

Fred had a job with Fielding Enterprises down in Meadville, as an entry-level engineer, making good money and coming up to see her every weekend, while Greg was only just graduating. Once he got his diploma, he would have to hit the pavement with the rest of their class and hope for the best. Of course, being a Fielding meant that Greg had more options than most graduates did. He couldn't coast on his name though. Greg knew that he had to keep his grades up if he ever wanted to make it in the Fielding family business.

The one thing that Susanna knew better than any of her close friends was that she needed to find the one guy capable of giving her a good life.

She had been denied that kind of life all during her growing up years. Her father had died before she was born, leaving her to the care of a struggling, single mother. Her earliest memories were of being shuffled from one neighbor to another so that her mother could head off to yet another of her low paying jobs.

Susanna vowed that she would never do that to any of her children and had worked as a babysitter and other odd jobs to pay for her college. Meeting "Fred," was her ticket out.

It was a dream come true when Susanna applied for and got the partial four-year scholarship. It meant that as long as she was able to keep working during her four years, she could pay off the rest and still have a small amount to send back to her mother.

Then, in her senior year, she locked herself in the bathroom, staring down in horror at the small plastic kit in her hand; the one that told her she was pregnant. It wasn't possible, but when a second, third and even a fourth all came back with the same devastating results, she almost panicked. She slowly took long, deep breaths, holding one hand protectively over her stomach. Once she had calmed down, she was ready to come up with a workable plan.

Susanna would tell both of the guys that she was dating, that she was pregnant. Whichever one agreed to marry her and raise the child with her, would be the one that she would choose. She would then break up with the one that was left. Her friends were appalled at such an idea and tried to get Susanna to see reason.

Oh, how she hoped that Fred would be that guy. He appeared to have the money and the job that she would need, since she couldn't exactly pursue or even keep a job of her own until she gave birth.

Susanna planned to have a quick marriage so that on graduation day, she would have a wedding ring on her finger to go along with the baby in her stomach. Maybe she didn't like the idea of being pregnant so young, but, at least she was sure that one of the guys would marry her.

Yes, that was exactly how this was going to play out, but fate has a nasty way sometimes of giving you what you want, but not exactly the way you want it.

She did end up with the rich guy, but it wasn't going to be Fred. He was the one that she told first, digging her nails into her other hand deep enough to leave gouges there that almost drew blood. She hoped against hope that he would reassure her that this would work out, that they would always be together.

In short, Susanna wanted that fairy tale ending that she had never had, and it didn't look like he was going to be the one to give it to her after all. Instead, Fred stared at her in shock and started to pace back and forth in his apartment for what seemed like forever. When he spoke, Susanna knew that her life, as she knew it was over.

"Um, I guess now is probably as good a time as any to kind of tell you the truth, Susanna."

The truth. That wasn't what she wanted to hear from him unless it was what she had been telling herself would happen all the way down to see him at his place.

All during the forty-minute drive, Susanna had told herself that Fred would see things her way. He would immediately offer her marriage. They would then have a quick and quiet wedding, the baby would arrive, and then they could move along with their lives as planned.

Sure, it would be difficult to be such young parents, but others did it all the time, conveniently forgetting the memories of her childhood. Growing up with a single mother had convinced Susanna that she would never do that to her own child.

That wouldn't happen with their child because there would be two parents, not one and he already had the good job. Once the baby came, she could get a job of her own, put the kid into daycare and they would be fine. Instead, what he told her had her staring back at him, anger filling her. How could he?

"I should have told you this when we first met but honestly, it wasn't a big deal and I thought you'd only go out with me because of my name, not who I am underneath.

I told my father when I applied here that I didn't want to be known as one of the Fieldings, and after a lot of serious debate, he gave in." Fred ran a hand nervously through his hair, making it stand up in tufts around his head.

"A Fielding. You're a freakin' Fielding and you never bothered to tell me?" Susanna was furious as she spit out her words

"Yeah, see, this is exactly why I didn't say anything at first."

"And just when were you planning on sharing this news with me?"

"Well, things kept going good with us, even with you dating some other guy and all and Susanna, I can't marry you."

"What? But, you're the father of this baby, you have to marry me."

"How do you know I'm the father? I mean, it could be the other guy's, right? You had to be sleeping with him too."

This was not how she expected this conversation to go. Fred was going to be the lucky father to her child.

This was why she approached Fred or Brad as he was really called, first. Susanna figured that once Fred proposed, she would call Greg, arrange for a meeting over coffee, and tell him that she was breaking up with him.

She didn't think he needed to know that she was pregnant, because she wouldn't be living in town any more and he'd never have to know. Brad. She had to keep reminding herself that his name was Brad, and not Fred.

However, he wasn't reacting the way Susanna had expected. It was bad enough that he wasn't the guy she thought he was with a different name and a completely different life. To top things off, he was now refusing to marry her.

"Maybe you should think about it a little, it's a lot to take in. We can talk more in a few days." She had taken a deep breath and tried to sound calm and reassuring. That's probably what he needed, time to think about it, think about losing her, as well as the prospect of losing his first child. Once he did, then he'd get over his nerves about marrying so young and they'd be able to make plans.

However, Brad shook his head and stepped back, away from her, his eyes showing regret and determination, which frightened her. If he still refused, Susanna would have to go to Greg. She did not intend to abort her own child, nor did she want to put the baby up for adoption.

"I can't, Susanna. I mean, you still don't know that I'm the father and I won't do that to some clueless guy who got caught up with..."

"Caught up with what, Brad? A whore? An easy lay?" Susanna practically screamed at him, she was so angry. "I see it now. You thought I was a cheap little tramp from the wrong side of the tracks that you enjoyed screwing. However, you can't possibly soil your precious Fielding blood with me now that I'm pregnant. Is that how it is?" She tossed her accusations at him, as she grabbed her purse and her coat and stalked towards the door.

"Don't worry, I won't ask you for one dime and you'll never see me or hear from me again."

She slammed the door in Brad's face and stormed out. She got into her car, narrowly missing hitting the telephone pole as she pulled into the heavy traffic, cutting off two cars as she made her escape.

It wasn't easy telling Greg, but he told her straight out that he would do the right thing and marry her. He didn't care if he was the father or not; she was the woman he loved and they would make it work. Greg gave her a small diamond engagement ring and seemed happy to be both engaged and a soon to be father.

As Susanna left her future husband and headed over to her mother's to give her the good news, she knew that she'd be seeing Brad at least one more time.

She, Greg, and her mother were invited to the family table for dinner, just the four of them, Brad not able to attend since he would be working out of town. They would spend that time planning a small, intimate wedding that would take place in two weeks. Greg's father had connections and was able to find a priest that agreed to perform the small wedding.

Chapter Eighteen

It all went according to plan with Brad staying as far from Susanna as possible until the wedding and then the two of them forced social smiles as they spoke which each other. Thankfully, all communications between them were limited to very brief exchanges.

It was only after returning from their honeymoon weekend that she learned where Brad had gone. It wasn't back to Meadville, but all the way across the country to accept an engineering job in a small town in Montana that she had never even heard of. He was working in yet another branch of the family business.

In the early years of raising Lucas, Susanna never once had contact, not even a Christmas card, with her brother-in-law.

Harrison, however, visited and often. He was delighted to be a grandfather, spoiling the boy as much as he could and spending time with the young family. Brad was the unspoken member of the family and Susanna never dared to ask Greg what he thought of his brother's repeated refusals to have anything to do with the rest of them.

It wasn't until Brad married Sylvie, that there was any sign of the ice starting to melt. She was born and raised in Montana, and so of course that's where their wedding took place which meant that everyone flew out on Harrison's private jet.

Sylvie was now a very happy person who was determined to mend what she saw as a rift, never once asking her future husband what caused it.

She was going to end that right here and now and her wedding day started things in the right direction. Even with all her efforts, it took several years of pushing and shoving at her husband to make it happen. When Devon was born, Sylvie knew that she had accomplished a great deal when they were named guardians for both children.

Still, there was more polite indifference between the brothers and Susanna. Sylvie's only regret now was that with the deaths of Greg and Susanna, she lost her chance to more to heal the family relations.

At least they were on their way to Erie. Sylvie promised herself that she would do what she could to help Devon through this terrible, terrible time.

Brad was grateful that he had married Sylvie. She was the best wife for him, even though he knew how disappointed she was that her efforts had never had the results that she had wished.

Nevertheless, how could he explain what Susanna had been to him all those years ago? How, even now, just thinking about her, made his stomach clench and his heart ache? Brad had loved the woman. He just couldn't marry her when they were so young.

That's why he refused, not because he didn't love her but because he did. If Susanna had asked for his opinion, Brad would have told her that he wanted her to put the child up for adoption. He still wouldn't have married Susanna though. They were too young for marriage but once the adoption went through, Brad was sure that Susanna would drop the whole subject of weddings.

He was barely in his twenties after all and he wanted to live a little first. Once he got all of that out of the way, then he would settle down to marriage and kids.

That last part of the plan didn't happen. After years of trying unsuccessfully for their own children, Harrison had recommended that Brad and Sylvie see a fertility specialist. Harrison knew the right physician and made all the arrangements.

After unsuccessfully trying a number of procedures, the specialist suggested that they try in vitro fertilization (IVF). According to Dr. Patronus, the fertility specialist, IVF was a procedure where Sylvie's eggs would be manually combined with Brad's sperm. The resulting embryo would then be transferred to Sylvie's uterus where if they were fortunate, a baby would develop.

Desperate for a baby, they agreed and underwent the initial testing. Unfortunately, the results from the testing showed that Brad and Sylvie could both have children separately but for some reason, her eggs would forever reject his sperm. IVF wasn't an option every time. Maybe in the future, there would be other treatments.

In the meantime, there was always adoption but both Brad and Sylvie decided against that.

Together, they had a happy, successful marriage; they didn't need children to complete them. Ironically, while they had long ago adjusted to life without children, they were about to parent an already grown child. The best part was that they had watched Devon grow up, at least from afar and she wasn't a baby or a small child. In fact, legally they only were responsible to her for a two-year stretch until Devon turned eighteen.

Brad and Sylvie didn't really know Devon all that well and now they were her only family. Without them and Harrison, she would end up in foster care, and that wasn't going to happen.

Therefore, here they were, back in Erie, and on their way to making that plan of Greg and Susanna's a reality. It had surprised Brad that he and his wife were named guardians of his brother's children though, especially knowing how Susanna felt about him.

Brad had long ago doubted that he'd ever have a chance to see them, let alone be in charge of their lives should anything happen to their parents. It had stunned him even more when Susanna was the one to break the news.

Every year when they flew across the country to Greg and Susanna's for the holidays, there had been an unspoken pact between Brad and his sister-in-law.

They were never to be left alone in the same room together for more than five minutes, and for years, they had both held rigidly to that agreement. However, as we all know, life moves on, and guards are let down a little.

As was usual for Erie, there was fresh snow for Christmas. Harrison had the brilliant idea of taking everyone outside, including the kids, to make a family of snowmen for the front yard.

Susanna begged off because she was fighting a nasty winter cold and felt too miserable to join in and Brad had been on the phone all morning with pressing work business.

By the time he had come downstairs and was looking around, everyone else was gone and he was alone with her.

"Um, where's the family?" He asked, nervously.

"They're all outside, making snowmen." Susanna pointed with one finger out the front picture window and walking carefully around her, Brad had looked out. He laughed a little as he saw the rest of the family, kids included, rolling the mounds of snow over to Harrison. It was his job of lifting each one. He then reshaped each form and put them together to form snowmen and snowwomen.

It was one of those rare days where the sun was bright. There was just the mildest of breezes and it felt good to be outside, breathing in the cold air and tromping around in the new fluffy snow.

Brad had stood there, watching them, and debated whether he should join the group. That's when he felt Susanna's presence beside him. He stiffened, much the way he always did whenever he saw her or heard her voice.

"Greg and I agreed that we want you and Sylvie to be our kid's guardians. You know, in case we die violently or something and they're still minors."

It was said softly in that way Susanna had, where you would strain your ears to listen to her. She only used that particular voice when she was trying to make an important point, like now, he supposed. Keeping their eyes averted from each other, Brad tried to match that casual tone of hers.

"Yeah? Whose idea was that?"

Susanna turned then, to take a long look at his profile.

137

"Mine."

"Yours?"

He turned to face her, and to say he was and looked shocked, was an understatement. Brad probably should have let it go at that, knew he'd most likely kick himself for not backing off and accepting what she said at face value.

He was never very good at that kind of thing. If he felt it, he usually said it, which had gotten him into a lot of trouble over the years, no question about it.

"Why would you suggest us? I know you hate even the sight of me."

Susanna almost recoiled from the bluntness of his question, and the obvious pain she heard in his voice. Her cheeks flamed for a few minutes as she struggled to try to find the right words to answer him.

"I guess this is the time I should tell you that I'm sorry, Brad. I am, you know, and not just for that scene we had when I found out I was carrying Lucas but for all of it."
She started to pace as the words tumbled out.

"I blamed you for the mess I found myself in, pregnant at twenty and alone like my mother had been. You weren't willing to take responsibility and I never forgave you for

138

abandoning me the way you did. I guess I kept punishing you."

"I loved you, Susanna." His voice was soft now, as if he was afraid to break whatever spell had been conjured that had led to this unfamiliar openness between them.

"I know, Brad." There were tears in her eyes and she brushed at them with the tips of her fingers, having been unable to find a Kleenex in the pockets of her jeans.

It was several long minutes later before he added.

"I still do."

Susanna acted at first as if she didn't hear Brad or maybe she didn't want to, but then she nodded, slowly.

"I know."

Then the spell was broken, as spells often are, by the opening of the front door and the shouts of glee from the family. Coats were tossed at the two members left inside.
Everyone began talking at once, as Brad and Susanna were hustled and manhandled into their outdoor gear and half dragged out of the house.

"You've got to see what we did."

"Mommy, come and look."

139

"I think it's a real work of art, Susanna. Come on out and bring your camera."

"Your kids are very creative, Susanna. You have to see what they came up with."

Grabbing her camera and slipping her feet into her boots, Susanna joined the others, stopping for a minute to look at how the snowmen were arranged.

There were the five larger mounds of snow along with two smaller mounds, all in their respective family units.

What really touched her was the fact that each one of them held hands, making them into one big circle. Brad caught Susanna's eye as he saw what she did. She half smiled back at him. Because of that smile, Brad hoped, that today would be the day for breaking the ice that had formed between them.

While that didn't completely work out, at least Susanna had stopped glaring at him or even ignoring him. They never did find time to spend alone again. Susanna saw to it that the time spent at holidays was spent with the entire family, no matter what the activity might be. Brad guessed that he would learn to live with that, even as he hoped with every holiday that he would get one more chance.

That would never be possible now that Susanna and Greg were dead. Brad's chance was over and he couldn't even share any of his pain with his own wife. Sylvie was very understanding and a wonderful woman, but she would never be able to accept that he had had a prior romantic relationship with his late sister-in-law.

The dead would remain dead. It didn't do anyone any good to try and change the past, no matter how much they might want to try.

That resolved he focused on his work. It had always been there for him, helping him through whatever personal crisis he might be facing.

Chapter Nineteen

It was hard to sit next to Brad after all these years and still know that there were questions left unanswered.

Sylvie kept busy with her phone, scanning through all the media reports that had hit the internet ever since the double murders were first reported.

Most were posts from people who only had opinions and some were pretty far out. There was the one that claimed Lucas was really a follower of Charles Manson, had been for years and that the murders were carrying out Manson's plan for world domination.

The world domination plot could be laughed off as the result of an overactive imagination, but the report that bothered her most was the one about the police. Someone had posted that they knew about the years of house calls for domestic abuse and claimed that Lucas had decided to put an end to it finally.

 There were many similar reports, each just as ridiculous and far-fetched as the next.

Of course, the partial media blackout that Harrison had managed to impose had done little to stop the wave of grisly stories being spread, despite his intentions to stop all the negativity.

It made Sylvie sick just to think of the mud that the family was being dragged through. She wondered yet again, just how Lucas and Devon were going to face all of these people. After a while though, surely Devon at least would get to live a normal life again.

The move to Montana would give the girl the best chance possible to do just that. It was how she planned to explain it to her niece in case she needed to press her advantage as her guardian.

The questions though kept nagging at Sylvie, small ones really but every time she came back here, they swam up to the surface, even with Susanna and Greg dead.

There was clearly no love lost between her husband and sister-in-law. Brad was always polite while Susanna did her level best to ignore him. They never touched, never exchanged any sort of greeting that Sylvie had ever witnessed and she had never understood why, not that she ever asked either one of them.

The kids and Harrison didn't seem to act as if anything was out of the ordinary so for the most part, she tried to let things be.

Sylvie got along well enough with Susanna though they didn't have an awful lot in common but, they could talk about current events and recipes since they both cooked.

It was a good thing though that they all traveled to Erie and to that big house of her in-laws to celebrate the holidays. There was plenty of room for everyone in the five bedrooms, four and a half bath house on two acres of fenced in lot. They only really had to pay for plane fare since they stayed with Susanna and Greg.

Sylvie helped out by making breakfast whenever they came to visit and she made a mean stuffed French toast if she did say so herself. Being with Lucas and Devon was often painful as it brought up her unfulfilled desire for parenthood, knowing that there was no fault here, not on either side.

If you couldn't have children with your husband, but most likely could with someone else, then there wasn't much you could do to change things and with no desire for adoption? Well, that meant that the issue was closed for all time.

Brad was still a wonderful husband and they had dealt with the loss of their parenting dream by creating a life that they both enjoyed.

Now that Greg and Susanna were dead, Sylvie doubted that she'd ever know what was behind the mutual dislike but there were worse things after all. With both of her own parents and even her stepfather dead, the Fieldings were her family, for better or worse. It was Sylvie's job to be supportive towards the kids and Harrison as well as Brad. That she could do.

She had always been convinced that she was born unlucky. That was what Sylvie had jokingly said every time she had anything bad happen to her. She had a string of ex-boyfriends, all of whom had done the breaking up part. They were sorry, but things weren't working out, maybe they needed more time. Yes, they had used the standard excuses. At first, Sylvie had believed them. However, that grew increasingly difficult when every one of them found a new girlfriend, weeks later. The breakups were bad enough. Learning that the guys had quickly found another girl was too much to handle. Sylvie tried hard to put it down to picking the wrong guys. It didn't always work though.

Jobs came and went too. She wasn't promoted, didn't get the plum assignments and whenever the recessions hit or other financial troubles, she was the first one let go.

The same went with apartments that were suddenly going co-op or being razed to the ground to build something else, and that included the houses she had rented over the years.

With each disappointing failure, Sylvie at least had her family to return to, but she was growing more and more desperate as the years went by.

It was hard to watch friends from high school and college snag the top jobs, get the best husbands, and start living the good lives.

By contrast, Sylvie went back and forth between what she called her temporary life and the real life back in the same bedroom she had had as a small child. Her mother and stepfather were worried too, though they never said as much, but money had always been lacking in that house.

Sylvie knew that when they died some day that she would have to sell the house just to make ends meet. There wasn't going to be anything left to inherit. However, her luck started to turn, slowly, so slowly that she still felt as if she were locked in a dream, one that she never wanted to wake from.

It all began on that one fateful day in late July when Sylvie was working as a waitress at yet another neighborhood diner when he walked in and sat at the counter. He ordered the special of the day, which on Thursdays meant meatloaf, mashed potatoes with canned green beans, all smothered in gravy. There were buttermilk biscuits with offerings of butter and jellies. You had a choice of anything you wanted to drink, though most had coffee. He had slowly eaten his way through his meal and had smiled each time Sylvie asked if he wanted anything else. When he paid his bill, he slipped a twenty in her hand as a tip, had winked at her, and then left.

She absently thought him a nice guy, someone probably passing through and promptly forgot him until he came back two days later and took the same seat at the counter.

This time when she served him, Sylvie asked if he was a newcomer or just passing through and flushed a little at her own boldness. The guy looked like a god with all that wonderful dark hair and those lovely brown eyes of his. He shook his head with a laugh and told her that it had been a little of both. He said that he liked the feel of this town and had decided to stay, not the least because of the pretty, dark haired beauty behind this counter.

That had made her laugh. Sylvie knew she wasn't beautiful and certainly this gorgeous guy could have his pick of beauties. He sounded sincere, so she joked back with him saying that he was only sticking around because of the great food that they served, which most knew for a lie. It was plentiful and hot but it wasn't exactly delicious.

That visit had set a pattern for Brad and Sylvie. Every Thursday and Saturday, he would come and sit at the counter. He always ordered the special of the day and joked around before paying his bill and leaving a twenty-dollar tip.

Sylvie didn't see him around town that much, but then she rarely went out these days, so that left the diner. After two weeks he asked her out to the local movie theater and to have ice cream and she knew herself to be falling for him and he hadn't even kissed her!

Brad told her quite honestly about the girl back home that he thought he still loved. He wanted to be fair to Sylvie, having learned his lesson long ago with Susanna.

Until that feeling passed, he didn't want Sylvie to think he was leading her on. She didn't care. She didn't care about the warnings from her friends that this was just another guy who'd end up taking her heart and then dumping her. Sylvie didn't even listen to her parents who thought Brad was much too good for her and told her so.

The day he proposed, exactly seven months, three weeks and four days to the very day that he had first walked into that diner, Sylvie thought she'd died and gone to heaven. Brad didn't want to elope, he said, but wanted her to have a real wedding, no matter how long that might take to arrange.

Sylvie surprised them both by gathering all her limited resources together. One month later, she was walking down the aisle wearing her mother's ill-fitting wedding dress with a bouquet of daisies and wild orchids. The only one to stand with her was her best friend, Tiffany, from the diner.

Harrison had insisted on paying for the reception after taking one look at the diner where his son and future daughter-in-law had met. His announcement brought everlasting joy to her parents. Even working three jobs, Sylvie's own family were unable to pay for a decent reception.

Harrison had made it easy, and had never acted as if his son had settled. In return for his acceptance, Sylvie vowed on that magical day when her life was joined with Brad's, that she would be the best wife he could ever want.

Chapter Twenty

It was a good sign that no one recognized them as they went inside the courthouse along with the rest of the morning group. They were just part of the crowd, which was a big relief. Sylvie tried not to flinch, seeing the story on the front page of the paper tucked under the arm of the man in front of her. He unfolded it to place it in the bin for security and she kept her eyes averted, afraid that she would burst into tears, which would be suspicious to say the least.

It was best that she follow what everyone else was doing even as she picked up her own bin, and started to put her valuables inside. The buzzer didn't sound for her or for Brad. That was a relief as she let out the breath she wasn't even aware that she was holding.

Brad scanned the directory and pointed in the direction that they had to go, making sure to keep his speed in her range. With their height difference, it was easy to forget that she had done a half skipping kind of walk in order to keep up with his much longer gait.

This time, however, they were in harmony as they knocked on Melissa's door in Protective Services a good ten minutes ahead of time. A blonde woman opened the door, inquiring how she could be of help.

"We're the Fieldings, Brad, and Sylvie, here for a ten o'clock meeting."

"Of course, right this way. Do either of you want coffee or a cappuccino? Your father brought in a machine yesterday and we've all been treating ourselves a little."

Her brown eyes danced as she spoke of Harrison. Both Sylvie and Brad declined the offer with a smile and a shake of their heads. The personal assistant led them inside, introducing them to Melissa and then closed the door behind them.

Harrison was already seated, with a cappuccino in one hand, which he placed on the desk to hug, first Brad and then Sylvie before sitting back down again and letting them take their own places.

"How was the flight? No problems I trust and I hope you two managed a decent night's sleep. As you can see for yourself, I needed a little pick me up." He lifted his cup in a half salute, sipping the delicious dark brew.

"Everything went smoothly, Dad, thanks. Maybe we can hit the exercise room later this afternoon."

"I'd like that, Brad. Good idea, though I have to warn you that the hotel has excellent training facilities. It won't be just a treadmill and a TV set."

Brad half laughed as he sat down. Knowing his father as well as he did, he'd be surprised if the hotel hadn't been selected solely on its available exercise equipment.

He had never known his father to scrimp on his exercise, having his own personal trainer and the results showed. The man might be in his sixties, but he certainly looked fit and more like a man fifteen years younger. It was an observation his father would be pleased with, not that he needed to be told.

Harrison conducted every aspect of his life as a man in control, who took advantage of every opportunity that came his way. It only added to the aura of power that surrounded the man. Even here in this small office, he exuded that power though Harrison also made it appear that he had permitted Melissa to run the show, without making the woman feel insulted.

Brad never learned how to be that smooth. It wasn't who he was and he was happy that one day his younger brother would be running the company. Brad didn't mind working in the business, he just didn't want to be in charge.

It was a sore point with his father and the only decision that he had made that sincerely baffled the older man. Brad knew that Harrison had already started working on Lucas and now that he was behind bars, well...., that plan was up in smoke, wasn't it?

What? What did he miss? He came to attention quickly. Melissa was speaking and he heard Sylvie gasp and start to cry.

"I'm sorry but what did you say?"

A small hand was on his left arm right away, his wife's way of showing comfort and support.

"Your nephew, Lucas, took his life yesterday morning." Brad turned to look at Melissa, staring at her as she spoke.

"Why wasn't I notified sooner? What the hell? Dad?"

Brad turned towards his father who had put his coffee cup down on Melissa's desk.

"We thought it best to wait to tell you this in person, and really when would we have had the time before now? You spent all yesterday traveling and sounded exhausted when you called to tell me that you had made it to the hotel. Was I supposed to tell you before you had time to refresh yourselves, so that you could spend a sleepless night?"

He heard the edge in his father's tone of voice and let out a sigh.

"Ok, Ok, but dead? How did that happen? Wasn't anyone keeping an eye on him?"

Melissa spoke up before his father could answer.

"I spoke directly to the public defender as well as to the detectives on the case. I can assure you that no one saw this coming.

Lucas was calm, seemed to be taking things well, and never once exhibited signs of someone about to take his own life. Believe me when I tell you that we're talking about three well trained staff members. It happened and I'm beyond sorry to have to be the one to tell you this. Before you ask, Devon has also been informed and set up with a grief counselor so we're on that as well."

This was not the easy part of her job but it was best to get it out of the way, before they asked to see Lucas. Melissa didn't want any unnecessary awkward moments nor did she want to just blurt it out first thing but it had to be done. The rest of the meeting's agenda depended a great deal on Devon now and her response to the fact that she was the sole survivor of her family. She would be the one needing round the clock surveillance but they would get to that.

Right now, Melissa wanted to discuss the particulars of the guardianship agreement and then they would bring Devon into the discussion. From the little Melissa now knew of Harrison Fielding, the funeral arrangements were already made, to take place the next day. Things were moving along fast, but the best thing for the minor child would be to get her new life started as quickly as possible.

Being in a state of limbo wasn't what Devon needed now. A change of scene as soon as could be arranged would help her process the grief of her family's horrible, violent end.

Devon had listened to the entire discussion and then it was her turn to express her own opinions and concerns. It was her family too. At first, she wasn't at all sure that she wanted to move from Erie to Montana. However, Brad and Sylvie assured Devon that this was in her best interest to start over in a new location. In the end, they all agreed though Devon still had a few concerns regarding her home.

"I don't want to go back there, to my old house. I can't do that. They can't make me, can they?"

She seemed so small, half curled on her chair as she buried her face into Sylvie's blouse.

"No, baby, no one's going to do that. We'll make sure that everything in your room is packed up and shipped on ahead so you don't have to worry about a thing."

Harrison had contacted a local realtor who was going to do a walk through at the end of the week. The woman believed that the house would be priced to sell and would do so right away. Despite the murders, the neighborhood was an excellent one and people didn't always shy away from that kind of notoriety. These days, a house in such a good neighborhood as theirs was prime real estate no matter what the history.

Harrison had already been given permission from the police to have everything boxed and shipped and had sent a few well-chosen moving men to do just that.

Sylvie was right when she had told Devon that her things would be waiting for her when she got to Montana. Harrison had supervised every possible detail and believed that the less contact the girl had with this town, the better. Devon had a few black dresses in her closet that would be suitable for the funeral so there really wasn't much else left to be done.

Chapter Twenty-One

Knowing that Devon was safe with Sylvie, Brad changed into exercise clothes and met his father downstairs in the recreation room. He was more than ready to beat out the stress that had been building the last two days.

"Did Lucas ever say why he did it?" Brad inquired.

Of course his son would ask, and who could blame him._Harrison didn't have the answers he wanted though.

"No, he never told anyone why, not even Devon, and you know how close the two of them always were."

Harrison was lying on the exercise mat, doing his bicycles, one series of repetitions on one side, the next series on the other side, when Brad walked in and joined him. The place was just as empty as it had been the previous day.

According to the girl at the front desk, most of the guests stayed overnight for a meeting or a concert, and they just weren't interested in exercising.

That kind of statement caught him off guard. Exercise was a vital part of his daily routine; keeping him healthy and energetic. Harrison knew that not many people were into physical fitness, especially not at his age. He could only hope that the tide would turn there, especially since Erie had such a growing number of fitness gyms.

Brad settled into place on the rowing machine, setting the timer and then getting his rhythm. This machine, the treadmill and the hot tub were the only parts he was interested in, no matter how much his father tried to persuade him otherwise.

"You believe her, of course."

"The girl doesn't lie." That one statement said it all as far as Harrison was concerned. His granddaughter was the kind of girl that told the truth, even if there were times when you might wish that she had kept her thoughts to herself. It would be interesting to see how she handled life in yet another small town.

"I thought it was funny when you told Devon that she could use her snow boots as fashion accessories. Come on, Dad, we do get snow in Montana, you know even if it's not in the snow belt like it is here in Erie."

His dad just laughed at that, even while moving on to another machine.

"Actually, I think she's going to find the move fairly easy, as both cities have a lot in common. The girl enjoys her fairs and museums and I hear that your town has a reasonable supply of both. I think she's going to do just fine with you and Sylvie.

In fact, I think it will be the two of you that will have to work on the changes.

By the time Devon starts college and moves out, you'll have to readjust all over again."

"She might just decide to go locally. We have an excellent university and she can still live in the dorms if she wants more freedom."

Brad didn't express his irrational fear that there had been a sickness in Lucas that would somehow infect Devon. Maybe it would inspire the girl to murder him and Sylvie. Brad still couldn't wrap his head around what made Lucas commit murder. Maybe Melissa was right and they would never get their answers. It was probably best to move forward.

However, it was sure to keep eating away at him. He always wanted answers, which was like his father. Neither man could leave well enough alone, but at least Brad knew better than to try to pester his niece. Devon had made it quite clear that she was just as confused and upset about all of this as the rest of them. Brad knew that he wouldn't get any answers from that source.

Brad shifted to turn his head, watching his father set up the treadmill for his programmed run. It was possible the cagy bastard knew more than he was saying. Nevertheless, he knew better than to try to bluff his way or even worse, to demand that Harrison tell him

159

everything. Neither approach was likely to work.

If there was anything more to be learned, it wouldn't come directly from Harrison and since only Devon was left, well, it was better to focus on the future instead of the past.

Did Harrison share that same fear, he wondered later as they both sat in the hot tub, a shared but comfortable silence between the two of them? One of the things about his father that Brad had always admired was the man's willingness to let his sons go their own way, to make their own lives, even though he knew that he had disappointed his dad by his continued refusal to have more responsibility in the family business. Since Greg had been the one to step up and do his part, Brad always felt he could concentrate on his own career, leaving everything else to his little brother. With Greg's death though, that meant that Brad was once more feeling the pressure, unspoken though it was between them.

"Dad, you know I can't take Greg's place." There, he had said it, and it was now on the table, again. Harrison sat there for a long while before saying anything, sat long enough that Brad almost started to squirm. The man had the patience of a saint and could wait out anyone, anywhere. Finally, though, after what seemed hours, he spoke, almost casually.

"Brad, I don't recall ever telling you that you were expected to take over for your brother, nor do I recall ever telling you that I had any expectations for either one of you, except to be the kind of men I raised you to be."

The man had always had a remarkable memory, so if he stated that he didn't recall an event taking place, especially a conversation, then it didn't. Brad never even considered questioning it. That was another one of Harrison's formidable talents. He was very good at remembering specific conversations. This ability worked equally well in business and personal relationships.
"I guess not. But I felt like I had to say it anyway, get it out there."

Harrison sat silently for a few more minutes, and then rose easily out of the tub, reaching for the warming towel to dry off before heading for the showers.

"In any case, we have the funeral tomorrow, the final arrangements for Greg and Susanna's household effects to handle. Then, we can all get on the plane and head back home. Oh, I took the liberty of inviting Aggie."

Aggie. That name sure took Brad back. She was the au-pair his father had hired to care for him and Greg. His mother had died shortly after his brother's birth, leaving Harrison with the necessity of finding live in help. Brad almost forgot about the young girl with the iron will. Despite her age, she had somehow managed to handle two small boys, helping care for them until they were old enough to be left on their own. He hadn't seen, yet alone thought about her in decades.

"How's she doing?"

"She's just fine. She's a grandmother now and widowed for the third time, but you can see for yourself tomorrow. I'm going to hit the showers before we have to meet the women."

Brad lay back in the foam for a few more minutes; letting memories of Aggie come back to him. He was too young to remember his mother who had died. The au-pair was memorable alright. Aggie was a young woman when she began working for the family. She took her job responsibilities seriously and managed to have some fun now and then too. From the time he could first remember anything much from his childhood, the memories included Aggie. If he closed his eyes right now, he could still conjure her up without any help at all. She had been a young woman somewhere in her twenties. What Brad most remembered were the bright blue, almost piercing eyes along with the blonde hair that she wore in a single plait down her back.

Aggie had been the one to teach them not just their reading and writing, but also their manners, doing so well that by the time the boys were in kindergarten, both could easily have sat through a six-course meal, using the proper fork and spoon, since she had made it a game for them. That was the secret, he supposed, of her success. She made learning fun and even got both of them into dancing around the kitchen sometimes, to what she called free style.

Aggie loved all kinds of music and the radio in those days played anything and everything from classical to country, to disco and even some rap. There were contests, prizes, and trips to museums and parks and the zoo, oftentimes in the summer, on their bikes where they learned how to stay out of the way of traffic and to keep close at all times. Then, almost before the boys knew it, they were deemed old enough to be on their own and Aggie was gone, on her way with top recommendations, to her next post, somewhere in Texas as he recalled.

Brad had wondered how she would fit in there and for the first few months at least, there would be a card, or a brief letter. After a while, even that contact was over, and their father was explaining that she belonged with another family now and that it was probably too difficult for her to keep in touch. Brad and Greg occasionally talked about her in the beginning, until Aggie became a mere memory, to be brought out now and then.

It would be good to see her though, see how she had changed. Doing the quick math, he realized that she had to be around the age of his grandfather and already on her third marriage. This he had to see for himself, wondering how the young, exuberant girl had matured, or had she just become older? It would certainly be interesting, and once more, he was struck with the pain that this was another experience that Greg would never have, that they could never share.

Brad had always wanted to know what happened to Aggie, but not this way. Oh hell, not like this. He could only imagine what she had thought once his father had tracked her down in that small town she had been living in the last ten years or so but she was coming. That was just like her though, to show up in a crisis. He bet she still had that calm way of hers which could help all of them.

Chapter Twenty-Two

"Brad?"

It was the same voice, which shouldn't have surprised him, but it did and yet it still brought him right back at the accompanying tap on his shoulder. The woman in question gave him a quick hug and then stepped back so that they could both take their stock of each other.

What Brad saw was a woman who had aged well, who wore her long braid up and wrapped around her head in one of those casually fancy styles that Sylvie would recognize even if he didn't. Aggie was still slender, wearing a black dress and black heels. The only jewelry she wore were gold studs in both ears, not even a watch. She carried a small black clutch and those fathomless blue eyes of hers held his as she took his measure, letting him speak first.

"You look wonderful, Aggie."

There was a smile on her face at the compliment, but unlike most of the women that he knew, she didn't say the usual things such as "Oh, you're too kind" and all of that nonsense. Aggie was always her own person.

"Thanks, you do too, though it's hard to see you all grown up like this." Her voice softened a little as she kept looking up at him.

"You and your brother were my first job as an au-pair; did your father ever tell you that?"

He shook his head.

"I didn't know that. So, did you answer an ad or sign with an agency?"

She laughed softly.

"No, actually your father saw me at the zoo where I was teaching a class. He thought that if I could manage to keep a group of four year olds entertained and under control, I could certainly work my magic on two small boys. He handed me his card and offered me a dream job." She paused, glancing over at Harrison who was deep in talk with a couple of people from the funeral home. "It was the best job I ever had, working with you two."

"You enjoyed us even when we drove you crazy? It's hard to believe that you got married and had kids of your own after you had to deal with us. Weren't we a walking ad for birth control?" Brad's tone was teasing. Aggie made it easy to talk to her and some of the tension he felt eased.

"No, smart ass." She lightly tapped Brad on the shoulder. "You two were great, just typical kids testing limits like you do when you only have one parent who's constantly traveling. How's he holding up?"

Her soft gaze went towards Harrison and then to Brad again, her voice soft and compassionate.

"We're all doing fine, Aggie. You know Dad. He can handle anything tossed his way; he's always been that way."

"Well, I'm going to take a seat, but I'll talk more to you both after the service."

She patted his arm and then went inside the church. Brad stood outside, waiting for Sylvie to come out of the restroom, before taking her hand and leading her inside to the front pew to sit beside his father.

From where they were seated in the church, two women caught the exchange between Brad and Aggie. They also kept watch as Harrison entered the church, making small talk with others who were still standing in the back of the church. Julia Jacobsen-Strong and Frannie Matthews-Williams sat as close to the family as they could. They had been long time friends of Susanna's and spent a great deal of time with both Lucas and Devon. Both had been shocked almost speechless when the murders and suicide news had come out in the press.

Each woman wondered if these deaths had anything to do with the secret that Susanna had entrusted to them so long ago.

"We'll find out more at the luncheon, Frannie. Don't worry.

I know how to ask questions without giving anything away. I **am** a partner in my family's accounting firm after all." Julia waved at Devon in the front pew, who waved back.

Frannie just nodded, only half listening as she waited for the signal that the mass was about to begin. She knew that Brad and Sylvie lived in Montana and had guessed that Devon would move in with them. As for the rest of it, she didn't know if bringing up the details of that secret would be a good idea. It might just make things even more difficult for those that were left. Susanna's father-in-law was a very powerful man. If he didn't want to talk to someone, then he could easily avoid them, though he had been warm and gracious with the two women, appearing pleased that they had arrived. They had even talked, briefly, with both Sylvie and Brad though there wasn't time to talk to Devon.

Ten minutes later the music started. Everyone rose; the funeral service for the three Fieldings had begun. Aggie sat there, listening to the readings, standing along with the others when asked to do so, and then she focused her attention on Harrison as he got up to give the eulogy, fighting back tears as he told the mourners about his son and daughter-in-law.

There were funny stories interspersed with those that made everyone think once more about the loss, and the fact that so many things would never happen now.

Lucas would never graduate from college; for him there was no promising future in the family

168

business. He would never marry nor produce great grandbabies for Harrison to spoil.

It made Aggie think again how lucky she was to have the life that she did, knowing how easily it can be snuffed out. Hadn't she already survived three husbands?

She wasn't an old woman either, but she already had grandchildren and two greats on the way which wasn't bad for a woman who was only in her late fifties and still looking good. She wasn't a fool; she had seen the appreciation in Harrison's eyes when they had come face to face after all these years. Aggie was retired but she still had a soft spot in her heart for the pair of two boys she had helped raise. She'd even had a mild crush on Harrison Fielding, though she was never foolish enough to tell him. That would have ruined things. Aggie was smart enough to keep those feelings silent.

There were secrets in that house though, and during the mass, Aggie wondered just what they were. They had to be significant enough for Lucas to have taken the way out that he had. Try as she might, Aggie couldn't come up with any guesses that made sense.

There were so many people here today. Most were neighbors and co-workers, but there were also a great many young people. They were likely friends of both Devon and Lucas, judging from the way they looked and it pleased her to see how crowded the church was.

Looking around at the others gathered there, she knew that they were probably wondering the same things. How does a young boy, barely of legal age, murder his parents and then take his own life? How could that be?

Aggie's daughter had said that with the boy gone, the secret, whatever it was, most likely died with him, but Aggie had her doubts. She reminded herself that she had never met Lucas or his mother and sister. Maybe the sister knew something.

It wasn't her place to ask questions, and knowing her place had been what had kept her working steadily all these years from one family to the next. She was the au-pair, the nanny, the helper. That's all she would ever be to each family, and it would be foolish to think that any of them would share confidential secrets with her. To them, she was just an employee.

Aggie wasn't any more than that and so it meant even more to have been invited here today. She suspected, however, that half of that reason was due to the scene that Harrison was painting for the media who had camped out across the street. Aggie had heard about the restraining order keeping the pack of wolves five hundred feet away from the family. She had also remembered blinking at the flash of lights that had snapped both her arrival and the greeting between her and Harrison.

Caring though Harrison was for his family, he could still use them for his own interests. At the funeral, for the cameras, he chose the role of grieving father and grandfather. He eased Devon from the back seat of the car she had arrived in, an arm wrapped protectively around her waist while he led her inside the church to a front row seat. Aggie had watched him greet everyone, a warm hug, or a firm handshake, whatever was required. Heck, she thought, he'd probably arrange for the media to learn of his putting flowers on the gravestones and manage to get that into print too.

The three men she had married over the years weren't that way. What they thought and felt was real and not for any show. She told herself that was how she wanted it.

Still, a man as polished and powerful as Harrison was not to be taken lightly. Aggie especially enjoyed how he looked in that black mourning suit with the subdued dark gray tie. It wasn't a hardship to have to look at him while he talked, watching as he wove his spell around the rest of the mourners.

At the end of the mass, the priest announced that while the Fieldings appreciated their presence, the luncheon to follow was to be a family only event. That news left both Frannie and Julia wondering what the real reason was behind such a decision. They had hoped for time to talk to Devon. Apparently, that wasn't in the plan. A few whispers from others were heard as the priest ended the funeral mass.

Once again, Harrison Fielding had made all the arrangements and he wasn't an approachable man for all the charm that he had displayed when the mourners had first arrived.

Have to give it to the old man, he gives a great eulogy. Look at my grandfather standing up there, talking about the three lives lost, all of that potential gone. Yeah, he's good like that, and the best part is that he really believes what he's saying. He's good at public speaking. See, that's the thing about him, he's really good at handling these kinds of things. I don't know who that priest is but at least I picked a good time to kill myself. Did you know that in the old days in the church a suicide wouldn't get a proper burial? This was only changed once it was pointed out by some smart ass that temporary insanity is enough to overturn a verdict, so why wouldn't the rule in a courtroom apply to a church? It was something like that.

Chapter Twenty-Three

Devon walked with the rest of the mourners outside to the back of the church where the cars were parked. It was only a short drive to the cemetery where they would lay her family in the Fielding plot. As her hand reached out to open the door to the backseat, a sudden breeze touched her hair and made her shiver, even though the day was already warm. A small smile came over her face and she said to herself, "Lucas is here." She had no idea where that thought had come from, so unexpectedly. She didn't believe in spirits, but it just felt like he was with her, somehow. Maybe he was, but more likely, it was just a breeze. Did anyone really make contact from beyond?

Devon looked at her aunt and uncle, and then her grandfather, not one of them appeared to notice anything. Already she'd seen a grief therapist; she didn't need a shrink to add to the list of appointments. Besides, by this time tomorrow, she'd be on the plane heading off to her new life.

The events of the previous days saddened her so that her eyes filled with tears. Devon mopped her face with a spare Kleenex, as she slid into her seat and put on her seat belt. Her aunt and uncle sat up front, as she quietly dabbed at her eyes, trying not to completely lose it. It was true that no one would comment if she started to bawl like a baby. Devon wasn't the only one hurting here today though.

It wouldn't be fair to any of them to force their attention on her, when there were so many other things that had to be handled, even if her grandfather had stepped in and taken over all the arrangements. She frowned, thinking about the holidays. Maybe she should bring this up now, when they were all together.

"What are we doing for the holidays this year?"

Her aunt turned partially around in her seat, a thoughtful expression on her face.

"I don't see why we can't all fly out to Chicago the way we planned, Devon. Don't you agree, Brad?" It worried Sylvie to see how composed the girl was, especially since she had gone through so much loss, but the fact that she wanted to talk about the future was a good sign, wasn't it?

"Sure, sure. Life goes on, doesn't it?" Brad sounded somewhat distracted as he steered the rental car through the busy morning traffic, careful to make the right turn.

He could never quite remember which road to take and then he saw Water Street up ahead. Brad got into the right lane and turned, heading past the ballpark and following the limo that was now two cars ahead of him. Fairview was a small little town, and he had almost forgotten that this was the cemetery, used for generations of Fieldings.

Everyone inside the car was quiet as Brad signaled left, waiting for the few cars to pass the entrance before making the turn. It was a small cemetery so it only took a minute or two to find a place to park along the side of the small pathway. Getting out, he helped first his wife and then Devon, walking with them both to where the priest and a few others were standing.

Harrison had arranged to have several chairs set up. He was already helping Aggie sit down when Brad, Sylvie, and Devon arrived to take their own seats. It was a small service and quickly done. When it was over, the Fieldings gathered beside their cars for a few minutes, while Brad talked to Harrison. He wanted to be sure that he knew which restaurant had been selected.

Of course, his father had even arranged for the private lunch at a local restaurant, one where they were less likely to be disturbed. Brad just nodded his thanks, and since he didn't know his way around like he used to, agreed to follow behind his father.

Lunch itself was a very quiet affair, with only the immediate family and Aggie. He had been surprised to see that the church was filled to capacity considering the situation. Brad had been even more surprised that his dad wanted only family at lunch. Maybe that was for the best. He certainly didn't feel up to making small talk with a lot of people and he didn't think that Devon could handle any of that either. Again, his father had thought of everything. He probably had planned his own funeral, which made Brad think that he and Sylvie needed to get that settled as soon as they got back home. It might seem a little morbid, but he wanted the task behind him. After all, it would be Devon having to do it all otherwise and that wasn't fair.

Then, even this was over and they were just four people, survivors of a major loss. The plan now was to head to the hotel where they would all spend the night. Brad and Sylvie were going to spend time at Presque Isle the next day with Devon, try to enjoy themselves a little before their plane left in the early afternoon.

They would all head to the airport together, even though Harrison had changed his ticket to a later time so that he could watch them take off before his own flight was scheduled.

Suddenly, almost before he had a chance to realize it, everything was finished. It had been a whirlwind of activity ever since Brad and Sylvie had arrived and now it was practically over and they were going home. Both women were communicating on their phones. Devon had hers returned to her as soon as the detectives had gone through it, and realized that there was nothing there to help with the case.

No one had any idea why Lucas had killed his parents, and had even less understanding of why he had then hung himself.

The police had the boy's laptop but it was locked. They were having a great deal of difficulty trying to figure out the code that would open it for them. The detectives had asked Devon about all kinds of things that Lucas had enjoyed; games, his music preferences, names, and even numbers. They asked her so many questions. Devon felt just as helpless and frustrated by her inability to be of any real assistance to them. In the end, they had promised to ship the laptop to her in a week or two. They had sent it on to one of their top men. If he couldn't figure it out, there wasn't much that could be done. The case was now closed anyway.

This was just a chance to get a few answers, though Devon doubted that her brother had left anything on his computer. Lucas didn't even give her any information that one and only time that they had talked at the courthouse. Even the public defender, Alice, had been unable to provide any clue that would point the detectives in the right direction. She had given Devon her card in case the girl ever wanted to talk. It was a nice thing to do, but Devon seriously doubted that she would ever make that call. Still, she tucked it inside her iPhone cover, just in case. For now, she was still trying to get a handle on what happened. Maybe one day a call to Alice would occur.

Sylvie finished checking her emails and texts with Glenda and several other friends, and closed down her phone. She smiled at Devon, trying to be upbeat.

177

"Do you feel like taking a nap when we get back? Or maybe we could watch a movie on TV instead?"

Devon looked up, frowning slightly. Her aunt was trying to make the best of a bad situation. It was her turn to make the effort.

She took a deep breath, wondering if that really worked. "I don't know, maybe lying down would be a good idea." Devon took another quick breath.

"I know this is hard for you Aunt Sylvie, finding yourself an instant parent of a teenage girl. I promise to be as good as I can be for you and Uncle Brad." She sounded earnest.

Sylvie put down her phone and put her hand on top of one of hers.

"Devon, are you alright? I don't deny that this is new for all of us but we'll work it out. We're family and families stick together."

Her aunt kept saying that repeatedly, kinda of like a mantra or something. Devon just wanted the numbness to go away. She had cried over the murders of her parents and her brother's suicide until she was sick to her stomach. It wouldn't bring any of them back. She barely felt anything now, somehow managing to get through the counseling, and the funeral. All she wanted was to get on with her new life and to leave all of this misery behind her.

Devon hadn't heard from any of her friends after the news about Lucas hit the media. She didn't know if that was because they had abandoned her, or if they didn't know what to say to her. It might have been a little of both but did it really matter? Devon was moving and she'd probably never see any of them again.

Maybe this was for the best, a kind of cutting of whatever ties she used to have so that she could move on. She lay down on her hotel bed, oddly soothed by those thoughts and closed her eyes. Devon let herself drift, falling fast asleep, when her aunt slowly snuck in to check on her.

It was hard on Sylvie to watch Devon have to handle such a monstrous turn of events. Not for the first time did Sylvie feel anger at Lucas for causing all of this horror and unhappiness. However, the moment passed quickly and then all she felt was guilt for these thoughts. Something had gone terribly wrong for Lucas, but she would most likely never find out what that something was.

If the police computer experts couldn't unlock his laptop, what hope did any of them have? Most kids and even her husband locked their computers, which wasn't such a strange thing. The fact that they couldn't seem to find the correct password was interesting. What could he have used that would be easy and yet just complicated enough that the experts were having such trouble figuring that out? Didn't most kids that age use a word or phrase to lock their computers or other gadgets? Lucas wasn't any different than a lot of eighteen year olds. They went with easy instead of using symbols and letters the way all the security experts suggested. Sylvie couldn't believe that this password was so complicated that it was stumping even the experts. Maybe Lucas thought he was a spy or something or maybe the answer was too simple. Either way, she tried to forget about that mystery for now.

Chapter Twenty-Four

"Aggie, I swear you look just as lovely as you did when I first saw you at the zoo that fateful summer day."

Harrison's green eyes twinkled over the rim of his wineglass as he toasted the slightly built woman sitting opposite. A low, husky laugh rang out as she tapped her glass to his, and sipped slowly; appreciating the crisp white wine, he'd selected to go with the Alaskan salmon. She was still slender at fifty-nine and pleased that her blonde hair was only showing a small amount of gray at the temples. It was braided and pulled back the way that she habitually wore it.

Aggie had taken great care with the rest of her appearance, applying a light touch with her makeup and even a quick brush of mascara on her lashes. Her black dress was cut to emphasize her shape and low enough in front to display a very ample bosom. Aggie flushed slightly, seeing that Harrison had indeed noticed.

"You always were a charmer, Harrison."

There it was again, his first name on her lips and he smiled, amused.

"What?" she asked in response to that smile, feeling more than a little flustered. She was glad to be only sipping at her wine.

"What can I say? You used my first name, Aggie. First time ever, in fact."

The smile on his face spread when she frowned a little.

"I'm sure that's not true."

"Oh, but it is.", he assured her as their salads were served. Harrison waited until she picked up her fork before continuing along that same tack.

"You always called me Mr. Fielding and here I am, only five years older than you."

"Well you were my boss, after all. I could never call you anything else. It wouldn't be proper." Aggie tried to focus on pouring her dressing and kept her eyes down on her plate.

"Ah yes, we must remain proper." He dug into his own salad, those green eyes of his still fixed on her blues.

"I like how you say my name, Aggie."

He topped off her wine when their salmon and baked potatoes were served. Harrison expertly steered the conversation toward easier topics starting with her other work experiences, which he then supplemented with funny anecdotes of his own.

By the time they had ordered dessert; a crème Brulee that she had always wanted to try, she covered her wine glass with a hand when he went to refill it once more.

"I'm not used to drinking so much and I need a clear head with you, Harrison."

He poured the last of the wine into his own glass and then picked it up, twirling the contents and watching her again, a more considered look in his eye that put her off guard.

"You've been married and widowed three times Aggie, and yet here you are, sharing dinner with me. We've kept in touch over the years, true enough, but this is the first meal we've shared that you haven't cooked and we're alone together."

Those last three words made her shiver, and she couldn't help it, even knowing that he noticed. Deliberately, she set her fork and knife down and for the first time that evening, really looked directly into those green eyes of his.

"Harrison, are you coming on to me?"

That smile came again, this time more feral than amused.

"I always said you were one sharp cookie, Aggie."

"I'm a widow now."

He reached across the table and picked up her left hand, his fingers brushing against the pale flesh where once three separate gold bands had encircled the ring finger. It was now left bare, as his eyes met and held hers.

"I know that. I'm also a widower, which means that we have no one to answer to." He paused long enough to make her even more nervous. "Do you realize that this is the first time all evening that you've actually looked at me? Why is that, Aggie?" His voice lowered. "Do I scare you?"

How could she tell him that she was more afraid of her own emotions than of him personally? He had never touched her like this before. In fact, the only physical contact that they had before were merely casual brushes of a hand here and there, until now. Aggie licked her suddenly dry lips, finding herself still helplessly staring back at him.

"Let's go. I'll drive you back to your hotel."

He dropped her hand and got up from his seat, pulling her chair out for her and helping her to her feet while he picked up the bill.

"Why don't you freshen up while I handle this, Aggie?"

She escaped, gratefully, to the ladies room, splashing cold water on her burning cheeks just as her cell phone began buzzing which made her jump, placing a protective hand against her racing heart. Her voice, when she answered though, was calm.

"Hi Brenda. Oh, I was just finishing my dinner with Harrison Fielding. Yes, the dead man's father. Catching up, you know that kind of thing."

She answered her daughter's questions automatically, promising that she'd be back in a day or two. They talked a few minutes more which calmed her. As Aggie ended the call, she felt more than ready to face Harrison and the perplexing and sudden desire she was starting to feel in his presence.

"Is everything alright?" Harrison appeared beside her, her coat held out as he helped her into it, then taking her hand, he led her out to the car and helped Aggie inside, letting her handle her own seat belt.

"I'm fine; I was just talking to Brenda." "My daughter." she added.

He briefly glanced her way. Chuckling, as he pulled into traffic, he nodded.

"I know who Brenda is, Aggie."

They were both quiet as he drove to her hotel. He parked then walked Aggie to her door on the second floor. Harrison stood there, waiting; his hands in the pockets of his overcoat, as she slid the card into the lock, then opened the door, while dropping the card back into her purse before turning to him.

"Invite me in, Aggie."

His voice was low and set off a clamoring need of frenzied desire in her blood, even while she inwardly struggled to fight the temptation that he offered.

"I really sh..."

His lips, warm and persuasive covered hers, while his hands cupped her head on both sides, keeping her in place. Stepping closer, he back walked her into the room, closing and locking the door behind them.

....

They had breakfast the next morning, on the terrace outside her room; both of them were bundled into complimentary bathrobes while they waited for room service. When it arrived, Harrison paid with a handsome tip and locking the door behind him, poured coffee for them both. He was smooth as he performed this small task, just as if he and Aggie had been together longer than only one night. Over the top of her cup, Aggie studied him; not a hair was out of place. Harrison looked as sinfully sexy as he did last night.

They had done things that she had only read about, wicked and wonderful things. Aggie felt virginal, instead of the thrice-widowed older woman who had experience in bedding men. Harrison might have been widowed only once, but he was clearly more adept sexually than she could ever have imagined. She had wallowed in the sensual pleasures, almost yet not quite begging for more.

Through all of that reckless night, he had been tender despite the wildness of how he made love to her. Wild, and passionate and tender; that was a combo designed to lower a woman's resistance. Aggie didn't even try to refuse him, not after that first kiss.

Harrison had undressed her slowly, letting his hands and mouth wander on a path over her naked body, until she was trembling against him. It was then that he picked her up, carrying her to the bed, where he ripped off his own clothes, his eyes holding hers in that all encompassing way he had.

Aggie was proud that she hadn't let herself go, but she knew she didn't possess the taut firmness she had from her youth. No amount of exercise and healthy eating was likely to give that back to her. Seeing the desire in his eyes was more than enough reassurance that she still was a sexy woman and so she allowed herself to let go. Aggie found herself completely submitting to him and the sexual acts that they were performing.

Aggie promised herself to relive every breathless moment later, but for now, they were returned to some sort of civility as they sat there in the early morning hours, enjoying the warmth of the sun.

They ate their pancakes and eggs in comfortable silence and when they began to talk at last, it was to make plans. Harrison knew that she had to return to Texas and he was needed back in Chicago. As they plotted and planned, it all seemed much too easy.

"It's decided then. You fly back to Texas and in two weeks, I'll join you."

Aggie started to protest instinctively but then caught herself and nodded with a smile on her face.

"Yes, Harrison. I'll need every day of those two weeks to set things in readiness."

Aggie meant what she said. Just prepping her daughter and sons would take some very skillful talking them around to the idea. Aggie's family had all heard of the Fielding family. They also knew that Aggie had worked for them during her very first assignment as an au-pair.

Once the news came about the murders, they all insisted that she fly back to Pennsylvania and pay her respects, which she had done. The difficulty now lay in explaining the change in her former relationship. No matter what words she used, it still sounded like a one night stand. Aggie though, was a firm believer that if you want something bad enough, you can have it and she **wanted** this.

Aggie wanted what she had found with Harrison enough to put up with whatever obstacles would stand in their way. A small part of her thought she could have an actual relationship with Harrison Fielding, and she wasn't going to give up the chance to try for it. Aggie's children were going to have to come to terms with this new man who was in her life, and if she was very lucky, they would welcome him.

"Good. I'll drop you at the airport later."

Aggie smiled at him, and went back to enjoying her breakfast, knowing that her life was about to change, maybe forever. She reminded herself that a woman who had survived three marriages knew something about men. It didn't help quell the butterflies still in her stomach to tell herself that she understood them, despite her numerous marriages.

A man like Harrison left her feeling out of her depth despite his efforts to make this easy for her. Aggie thought she knew what was going on here; they had wanted each other and they had made love for most of the night. In his world, this was likely just another affair; one in a long line of affairs a worldly man like Harrison had experienced. He'd sate himself with her until he grew bored, then he would give her a lovely and expensive parting gift before moving along to the next woman. She tried to tell herself that a man like Harrison could leave her with a broken heart, if she persisted in wanting more than he was willing to give. On the other hand, she wasn't about to give up that easily.

As if he could read her thoughts, Harrison put down the paper he had been reading and just stared at her. Aggie felt the blush come back to her cheeks, as she told herself that for once, the consequences be damned. She was going to have that adventure with this man. For so long, she believed him to be out of her reach. Aggie had him now in her bed and she intended to do whatever it took to keep him there and interested for as long as she could, before he ended things between them. She told herself to guard her heart before she ended up hurt and alone.

For himself, Harrison had never had a woman with the earthy surrender and eagerness that Aggie had shown him in bed. She fascinated the hell out of him with her rules for living, while abandoning herself to him in a way that no other woman had quite been able to do. Maybe that was because his former choices had been skilled enough to give him what he wanted, and then were just as willing to move along.

He had usually selected as his bedmates, women who were no more interested in having an actual relationship than he was. Harrison had no need to remarry. He already had two sons, which was the only reason he had married the first time. When his wife died, he was left with two healthy sons and a very wealthy dowry and could pursue any woman that caught his eye. Harrison was content to continue the way he always had. He kept fit so that he could keep up with his younger lovers, even as he had learned the hard way to never sleep with a woman who wasn't on birth control.

That meant that he frequently narrowed the field to that of married or engaged women. He preferred those who were looking for adventure and excitement. A baby for any one of those women would have been the ruin of their lives.

Aggie also appeared to fit his agenda, though he knew from the very first touch, that she was different. It was going to be exciting to learn more, Harrison thought as he ran a finger up her hand to tickle her inner arm before pushing back in his chair and getting out of his seat.

Aggie knew what he wanted and she eagerly got up as well, untying the knot in her robe as they walked back towards the bedroom. It was a good thing that she wanted it too.

Chapter Twenty-Five
Several years in the past....

The one night stand had been a poor choice. He woke up the next morning, lying in bed beside a woman who was twenty years his junior. She might be even younger because he doubted that she had told him the truth about her age.

In any event, they had met in an off campus bar, a place he frequented from time to time. He liked going there because it reminded him of his college days.

He had gone out on that fateful night to have a quiet drink and maybe a light flirtation. It was another, usual, night for him until the girl approached and sat beside him at the bar. What struck him most aside from the youthful good looks and long dark hair was the air of confidence she had about her. She smiled as she sat down and ordered a mineral water, until he had lowered his voice and whispered

"They don't card here in case you're interested."

She smiled again, changing her order to a beer and then swiveled her chair around to face him.

"Thanks. I've never been in here before and usually there's a list of what places card and which don't."

She hadn't offered him a name, and he didn't either as they struck up a conversation. It started out light and teasing but as the beers kept coming their talk grew more sexual. The talk was so sexual in fact that the girl had suggested that they go somewhere quieter. He had responded quickly, even eagerly by paying the two tabs and helping her off her barstool and into her coat.

She had walked to the bar. This pleased him as he helped her into the small little sports car, driving the two and a half blocks to the nearest hotel. Once inside the room, he had pressed her face to the wall, while he quickly undressed her. He tossed her clothes onto the small chair by the window, his fingers sliding deeply inside her eager and wet body.

The hours they spent exploring each other that night had been intensely sexual and mutually satisfying. With their age differences, he was much more skilled about how to please her than she was in pleasing him. Still, she made for a creative and enjoyable student. The best part was that he was sure they'd never see each other again. The pleasure he had given her would mean that she'd remember him years into the future, all without ever exchanging names.

That part was very accurate, as she not only remembered him, he remembered her when next they met. That was the one time when he had almost lost everything that mattered in his life. Only his great skill and the warning look that he had sent her, had saved the day, or so he thought.

Back to the present, yet again....

After the last of the hugs goodbye, and the frantic rush to the plane of many passengers, Harrison simply stood at the main window in the airport. He watched as the planes cruised down the runway and then took flight. Harrison continued to stare until his own flight had been announced. There was no need to hurry. He had plenty of time. This was a small airport even if it did have the "International" label attached to it.

Harrison easily strolled over to the ticket counter, presenting his ticket. He had already been cleared earlier along with the rest of the family. As he settled into his seat and fastened his belt, he leaned back, his mind already shifting into business mode. He would land early enough to get in a good work out and a steam. Harrison planned on an early night before facing the mountain of texts, calls, and faxes that needed his expertise.

He was more than ready to tackle the complex business waiting for him. The work he had done for the funerals and the rest of the arrangements were easy enough, yet there wasn't enough challenge for him. He was a man who thrived on the difficulties presented in his daily world.

Harrison would see them all again in a few months for Thanksgiving, and then again for Christmas.

Devon would continue her offhand and occasional texts, which would no doubt increase as she adjusted to her new surroundings.

They all had to move forward now. That was for the best and they had all agreed. Somehow, he knew that it would be easier said than done. Family. Harrison gave himself a mental shake. More trouble than they were worth, most of the time, even with his who had given him so few headaches. Two murders and a suicide was more than just a glitch in the system.

It still irritated Harrison that Lucas had never once tried to contact him. Sorrow lined his brow at the loss of his son and daughter-in-law. Yes, he felt sadness over Lucas' death but he was also angry and perplexed. How could this have happened? The only one with answers was lying in a coffin next to his parents. It grieved Harrison more than he had expected.

He wasn't the kind of man to let his feelings show but he was deeply troubled by everything that had occurred. It wasn't the scandal that bothered him. It was the tremendous loss of so many.

Harrison wasn't prepared for the multiple deaths, and fully expected that he would be the one to go first. That's how it worked. The older members died before the younger ones and never due to murder.

His thoughts drifted briefly back to Marjorie Gold, the girl he had married at twenty-two. She was a placid young debutante who meekly did the bidding of her parents by marrying into the illustrious Fielding family. She remained calm and biddable to an end that had come suddenly and without any warning. One minute, he was holding his second newborn son and the next minute, he was ushered from the room. The doctors worked frantically to stop the massive bleeding, but were unsuccessful in saving Marjorie's life. She was pronounced dead exactly fifteen minutes after giving birth.

Harrison had never been in love with the girl, yet he had still grieved her loss. It had been a most advantageous marriage. Even after death, her family had dutifully turned over the rest of her inheritance. Marjorie had lived up to her side of the deal in producing two sons before dying, leaving the three males alone to somehow carry on together. Harrison put aside his own grief to quickly hire an au-pair. Then he got on with the running of the family business. He never remarried though he had enjoyed and still did, numerous liaisons with very eligible and entertaining women, none of whom he had the least desire to wed.

Marriage was more often a burden, he felt, instead of a true pleasure. Harrison had to admit that it was good that Brad had Sylvie to help him and Devon. If Devon had come to live with Harrison, he would have hired a housekeeper or a live in companion. Still, Devon had planned to attend Smith in two years and Harrison intended to help her to do just that.

The girl was easy on the eye, smart and had a pleasing personality. It didn't hurt that she came from an influential family and he planned on her taking her rightful place in society when the time came. Already, thanks to his continual efforts, Devon had been presented shortly after her sixteenth birthday. The coming out event into proper society had taken place weeks before young Lucas had taken out himself and his parents.

Harrison had needed all of his charm and contacts to smooth that over so that Devon wouldn't suffer for the association. He had even toyed with allowing her to use his wife's maiden name of 'Gold', but knew how strongly Brad would protest.

No, it was better to have the girl present herself front and center and to face what had happened. It would strengthen Devon and make her even more of an asset, at least as far as he was concerned. Now, all he had to do was continue to nurture their relationship and keep the girl on the right path. It would be all the more tricky with such a distance, but in some ways, it was actually easier. He had done so much for her and her brother and it was time that he was repaid for all of his efforts, behind the scenes, so to speak.

His eyes darkened slightly, but hearing someone approach and say his name had him smoothing over that darkness with his usual charm, as he consented to enjoy the drink that was presented.

The young airline steward was nubile and very fresh. She was also very unacceptable for more than a casual flirtation. He had no interest in wasting himself on a woman who could bring nothing more to the table than perhaps an enjoyable romp in bed. Once Harrison was walking off the plane, her name and face were already a mere memory.

He had other fish to fry, so to speak, and he was going to enjoy himself, now that he was back in town. His car was waiting, his personal assistant at the ready to load the suitcase and laptop in the trunk before opening the door. There was the usual update given and minutes later, he was back at his own home, having given the assistant the rest of the day off. They would meet up first thing in the morning.

 The security system turned off and then reactivated behind him, Harrison headed for the lower level where his personal gym was set up. Stripping down, he pulled on a pair of work out shorts and a T-shirt. He then changed his black loafers for a pair of top of the line running shoes before getting down to his routine. Harrison started out with a series of stretches, before reaching for the weights. Following his trainer's carefully written instructions, he moved easily through his workout, ending as most of them did with a run. Today, it was a long run of thirty minutes, followed by a twenty-minute steam in the sauna and a cold glass of white wine. Harrison showered and changed into a casual pair of blue jeans and a sweater before heading upstairs to the gourmet kitchen.

Thanks to the pre-chopped vegetables already in the refrigerator, he made up a salad and grilled a lean steak, topping off the meal with a half a glass of red wine. He had programmed a classical musical selection that helped him to relax.

Harrison still had work to do in order to be fully prepared for tomorrow and the rest of the night was spent in his office. At precisely eleven p.m., he shut everything down. He was a man of strictly ingrained habits and he had lived alone long enough that he saw no reason to even try to change any of it.

Harrison Fielding enjoyed being exactly who he was and he planned on living a very long time, to see to the rest of his plans for his family, through Devon. As his eyes closed, he began to sort through the possible families that would benefit from an alliance with the Fieldings.

Chapter Twenty-Six

One Month Later. In a small town in Montana...

The newly redone bedroom in pinks and lavender was a teenage girl's dream. There was a large canopy bed on one side and a small set of bunk beds on the other. The walls had been sponge painted a softer pink with light tendrils of even softer lavender and were almost completely covered by a collection of black and white photographs; the only box of her mother's that Devon had opened. The prints tended to be outdoor shots; her personal favorite was the winter scene down at Presque Isle at sunset. The picture had explosions of dark orange and reds, showcased with pure white snow that lay untouched by any footprints.

Susanna had been quite a skilled photographer and though she preferred the neutral monochromatic palette, there were various family shots done in color. These were scattered on every available surface of her room, except for her desk. Devon felt uncomfortable having the faces of her family staring at her every time she took her seat. It felt somewhat spooky, having the faces of her dead family that close. Maybe one day she'd be able to look at them, even go through a few of the family albums. It was too soon for any of that right now.

Her Aunt Sylvie had added a large white, pink, and lavender throw rug with matching fluffy pillows for her bed. The room was as girly girl as possible. The large white screen to block off parts of the room that contained clutter complemented it.

That part was funny because Devon was a most annoying female. She was a neat freak. The screen was a solid white dotted with pink and lavender flowers on wheels so that she could move it wherever she wanted, just to change things a little. Most of the time it stood in front of and around the small white computer desk, which faced the large window, so that she could look outside whenever she wanted to.

The only requested additions were the multiple organizer boxes cleverly placed in nearly every conceivable space around the room. The other window was smaller, faced the side of the house, and in a small nook in the one corner stood a large, somewhat ornate round mirror on wheels. The mirror had been a welcome to our home present from Devon's aunt and uncle, and even now, it brought a smile to her face every time she looked into it.

The rest of Susanna's personal effects were in a total of twenty-nine individual boxes and crates with several garment boxes under her bed and on the top shelf of her walk in closet. Aloysius sat in splendor on a pink and lavender ice cream parlor chair that sat at the footboard of Devon's bed.

So far, she hadn't been able to force herself to open any of the boxes. She couldn't handle going through any of them even with Aunt Sylvie's offers to help. It felt reassuring to Devon, to have all of this in her room. One day, she'd be ready to go through them, but not now.

As far as her father's personal possessions and their distribution went, those decisions Devon left to her uncle and grandfather. Harrison went through everything, keeping a few items for himself, donating what was left to the local thrift store. Her Uncle Brad didn't want anything; he was happier without the physical reminders of his brother.

Her former home had sold rather quickly even though the new owners had been told about the double murders. The buyers weren't fazed about it; they had watched the media reports too. What they did instead was call in a shaman to have the house cleaned and then moved in immediately after the closing.

Once the new owners moved in, it meant that Devon could never go back for one last walk through, and maybe that was for the best. The psychologist she was seeing was helping her to understand that for many people, these kinds of tragic events were too much to handle. The doctor left it open that maybe when they grew older, they might reach out to Devon, but she seriously doubted that would ever happen.

Devon was working now on how to tell a true friend from a false one, and hoping she'd make at least one that would be there for the long haul. The rest was better left forgotten.

On a cool but sunny Saturday in September, she sat on her bed, her legs curled under her jean clad form as she hesitated, one hand on the small packing box, her teeth worrying her bottom lip.

It was a habit she was mostly unconscious about having. Devon only did it when she was nervous like she was at this moment. What would she find in that box? Would there be secrets revealed? Would this be a waste of her time? Devon lifted her eyes from the box and scanned her room, again.

There were several piles already on her floor, the largest one being the discard pile. There were clothes, and games and all kinds of things from her brother's closet that fit neatly into four large crates. Eighteen years and this was it?

Struggling with her nerves, Devon forced herself to ease the top off the first box before dumping the contents all over the bed. Aunt Sylvie left trays of food outside her door, so that Devon could handle this by herself. She had gone through the other boxes and there wasn't much in them worth saving except for a few of his art projects.

The only other item of interest was Lucas' ratty old high school basketball jersey. Devon was keeping his jersey, but she threw out the art projects.

She started picking through the pile on the bed, automatically sorting and discarding until she came down to the last few items.

Lucas's iPod. Strange but Devon thought he carried it with him everywhere. Lucas never let her see what songs he had on it and now was as good a time as any to find out for herself.

She slipped her own ear buds out of her back pocket, fitting them carefully in her ears as she turned it on and took a listen. A smile crossed Devon's face as she heard familiar tunes that had been downloaded by John Legend. Devon had introduced Lucas to this artist and then for some reason or other, stopped listening herself. The song currently playing was the one about his new bride. It made her close her eyes, listening and remembering the video that went with the music. For the millionth time, Devon wished that she would one day find a guy who loved her enough to write a song about her...

Then she half rolled her eyes at how stupid that sounded, but why not wish for the moon? Devon scanned through the rest, nodding as she found a few by Michael Jackson, Maroon 5, Clean Bandit, and Ed Sheeran among others. Lucas' favorite song by Adam Hood, called *"Million Miles Away"* that he had loved so much was there as well.

When she was done, she learned that Lucas downloaded entire albums while she went with individual songs.

Maybe it was a girl thing; but Devon's choices were what her mother called 'separates'. Lucas never understood how Devon could only upload one song, and she never understood his need to upload the entire album. He tried to explain that it might be that one song that got him interested in an artist, but he knew them better by listening to the whole of his music.

She also found it hard to understand how Lucas could like pop, rock, rap, country and even a few classical songs. Devon mostly liked pop and rock and that was about it.

There was the letter from MIT and she read it aloud. Devon's eyes filled with tears, remembering how excited all of them were about his acceptance, and a little sad. Well, at least she was sad, though she knew she should be happy for him and she was, really. However, it meant that Lucas would be leaving her; that's all that kept running through Devon's mind. Lucas would be leaving her and starting a new life that she had to hear about from afar. Devon had a secret wish to have her own adventure, but not in this way.

Now, in a few short days, she'd be attending high school as the new girl. As if that wasn't scary enough, she knew that even in a small town, the other students had to have heard all about the double murders and suicide. Devon had to give it time.

She knew that, deep down inside, she really did, but knowing something and facing it were two very different things. Devon would have to take that next step by herself. She was taking a school bus for the first time. Both her aunt and uncle had offered to drive her, but she was going to take the bus as every other kid in town did.

Devon would walk through the front door, find her homeroom, and get to all her classes on time.

There had to be other new kids, maybe they'd all hang out together, or maybe she'd be alone, shunned because of what her brother had done. Devon was fine with that too. This was just high school; it wasn't the rest of her life. It was only two years and then she could go anywhere she wanted. She still thought she wanted to go to Smith when she graduated.

Devon knew that she could tough it out if she had to. She was a Fielding and they handled what came their way. What she really wanted though was a friend or two who would be there for her from the first day, even if that was too much to ask for. She still wanted that, no matter how it might sound.

"Devon, I can have dinner on the table in five minutes. Do you feel up to joining us?"

Aunt Sylvie was very considerate of her privacy, always knocking, never just opening the door and sticking her head inside, and not asking her too many questions.

She was the one who had shown Devon around the town. She even bought two second hand bikes so they could take a few rides around the Clark River. They all attended a Labor Day picnic in the park, enjoying the music and each other's company. The people in this small town seemed friendly and welcoming, but Devon was still nervous. It wasn't like she didn't have a lot of baggage, to use her mother's term. Devon had more than she could possibly handle. She also had her father's strong spine.

If anyone caused trouble or tried to, she would ignore them, or walk away. Devon would just have to see for herself how the kids would act. Would they mirror their parents, or would they reach their own conclusions? Maybe it would be some of both.

"Sure, Aunt Sylvie, just let me wash up."

"Ok then, I'll see you downstairs."

Devon could tell from the sound of her voice that her aunt was in a happy mood. She knew it was because she was trying to be cooperative. It was what everyone wanted, and Devon didn't want to act sad.

She didn't want to **feel** sad either. She wanted her old life back, which wasn't going to happen, but she could try for happy. Less than five minutes later after quickly splashing water on her face and combing her hair and she was downstairs. There was a wonderful and familiar scent in the air of spaghetti and meatballs along with the made from scratch sauce that her Aunt Sylvie made.

Devon helped put platters of food on the table. They all sat, holding hands for a quick blessing before passing everything around. A few stories, even jokes were exchanged before they started eating dinner. She knew it would take time before she could ask her uncle if he would share stories about her father from when they were kids.

Now wasn't the right moment, Devon knew that. There would be sad times when all they could think about were their personal losses. They would have to work through it to get to happy.

That's what all parents wanted, wasn't it? They wanted their kids to be happy. While she was eating and expertly twirling her pasta around her fork, Devon watched her aunt and uncle.

They took to this whole parenting thing so easily. Of course, Devon's being older made it easier, didn't it? With a baby, they couldn't even communicate when you brought them home. With teenagers, they came all put together with thoughts, opinions, experiences, and even values that might be different. She knew that they'd have to struggle through it together as she helped herself to a second serving.

Chapter Twenty-Seven

Devon knew that kids in different parts of the country dressed differently. In preparation, she had spent the weeks prior to school opening, shopping with her Aunt Sylvie. Both of them kept an eye out for what other girls her age were buying. Devon didn't want to be a clone; she just wanted to fit in. It didn't take long before they had both settled on a look that would work; more of a casual yet girly appearance that best suited Devon's basic looks and personality.

Now, all she had to do was get on the bus when it got here. She hoped that at least one person would talk to her. While she waited, two girls joined her at the bus stop. They stared at her for a few minutes. The pretty redhead with braces, approached with a friendly smile.

"Hi, I'm Mandy. You must be the Fieldings' niece. I live across the street, four houses down." She pointed in the general direction.

"This is Chloe, and she lives right next door to me, which is about five houses down, I think. You live in the brick house, right?

Devon nodded, vaguely remembering what the other houses in the neighborhood looked like.

"I'm Devon and yes, I'm their niece."

Chloe, a brunette with short hair that hugged the nape of her swan like neck, just stared until

Mandy nudged her. When she spoke, it was in a soft, kind of raspy voice.

"Sorry about that. I think I saw you over in Target last week, buying school stuff, right? You and your aunt were hanging out."

"Yeah, we bought some stuff, you know how it is."

The girls kept talking until Devon felt more at ease. When the bus pulled up, they all got on together, with her pausing by the driver, unsure of what to do next.

"Dev, back here. We got a seat saved."

Devon smiled in relief at Chloe's yell from the back of the bus and headed their way. With every step she took, she could feel the stares and whispers that were following her. She knew she'd have to get used to the scrutiny. Not only was she the new girl but she had that past that everyone must have heard about by now. If they didn't, they would learn soon enough.

Once the bus unloaded in front of the high school, her new friends helped her find her locker, and then her homeroom. As it turned out, Chloe was also assigned to the same homeroom. Devon already had her schedule, so both girls looked at what she was signed up for, checking it against their class listings. Mandy had three with Devon, while Chloe just had one.

Fortunately, all three girls took lunch at the same time.

Chloe even did a quick drawing of how the school was laid out for her, and walked with her to their very first class, introducing her all around. The school was larger than the one Devon had gone to back home. Most people seemed more curious than anything and she liked to think that had more to do with her being a new face, which wasn't that common, according to Mandy.

"Last new kid we had was when? Back in grade school and they didn't stay more than a few months. Kid was an army brat." She was walking along with Devon as they headed to lunch, knowing that Chloe would save those seats. It was already a little past noon and Devon was starting to feel much more at home here, like she actually belonged.

She liked that she was going to a school with an eagle as its main name. Devon even thought it clever how they used that name in their belief statement. Of course, it also included the standard line about exploring your possibilities, acceptance of differences and diversity, and open mindedness. It even promoted how to excel through academics, arts, activities, and giving back to the community.

The principal and guidance counselor were impressed by Devon's academic background and seemed willing to be helpful. The first sign of that was arranging regular meetings with the school psychologist, who was just as friendly and good at putting her at ease.

The high school had a strong academic program to help develop all aspects of her educational life, especially learning how to work and live in the globalizing world they were now facing.

Devon found it interesting that there was so much emphasis on fitness as well as agriculture. The list of class selections was just overwhelming. If it weren't for the help of the guidance counselor, she'd never be able to make any decisions. Together, they had pored through the list of offerings, using Devon's own background and interests to help set her on her path. They finally agreed on one that was just challenging enough to keep her interested without feeling in over her head.

This might be a small town, like the one Devon had just left, yet education was a big deal here too, so that at least was familiar.

The food they served in the cafeteria was pretty much the same too, but it seemed to taste better. Mandy told her that was because most of the stuff came from the local farms.

"Me? I'm not much for fresh fruit and veggies but its part of the menu and so, what the heck, you know? They also make a mean veggie burger or even a moose one if you want."

Devon just shook her head.

"I'm still trying to adjust to living here. It's easier if I stick with food that I recognize."

"So, must be strange knowing that half the kids here are dying to ask about the killings."

Mandy just gasped and sent Chloe a look, but the girl just shrugged her shoulders.

"I'm only saying what everyone's thinking." Chloe smiled at Mandy though. She turned to Devon, all eager and curious. "You don't mind, do you?" If there was one thing that she had learned since this nightmare had begun, that was how to spot nasty and gossipy people and Chloe didn't fit. Devon finished the food in her mouth and took a sip of her milk.

"Look, I know everyone wants to talk about the murders and suicide and maybe someday, I'll be able to, but right now, I just want to feel normal again."

Mandy nodded, still shooting Chloe looks.

"I get that. It's why I didn't say anything as mean as my friend here. But, Dev," her look was sympathetic but not overly so.

"People are going to ask and well, they might not give you the time you think you're going to need. I'm just trying to warn you, you know?"

Devon did know. That was the point. She was well aware that at some point in time, the new people in her life were going to ask about her

past. She would have to think of what to say
without bursting into tears all the time. Still,
she just shook her head.

"Well, if anyone asks, that's what I'm going to
say. I'm not ready yet. I don't know when I'll
ever be ready."

Chapter Twenty-Eight

Three months later...

Christmas:

They'd kept their promise to her, thought Devon as she picked up the large crate simply marked "Christmas" in her mother's writing and sat down with it on the floor of her room. She thought back to her first holiday since the murders.

With her Aunt Sylvie and Uncle Brad, she had flown to Chicago to visit her grandfather for Thanksgiving. It was the first test, to see how holidays were going to be and it was tougher than Devon had thought it would be.

Sometimes, all this caring stuff felt smothering yet she didn't want to say anything. Devon knew that the rest of the family had suffered too. Their own grief was still there, as they gathered around the table in her grandfather's dining room. It showed in their eyes and in the way they pretended to eat their holiday meal. They'd picked at and just pushed their food around their plates. Still, they were together, as a family.

Devon's therapist had warned her not to expect too much.
She got it but she missed her parents and Lucas more than ever. She kept telling herself repeatedly that the first year of every holiday was going to be the hardest. Isn't that what

everyone told her? It sure seemed that way and now here Devon was, staring at this box, trying to will herself to open it.

Back in Erie, there would be the annual hunt for the perfect tree that her father and brother would chop down and bring back to the house.

Back home, Devon and her mother would open all the decorations and ornaments and get ready for the next step. Together, the four of them would put the tree up, and place each ornament, every strand of lights, every foot of tinsel.

There would be the mock fight over who would get the honor of putting the battered angel on the very top. Their grandmother on their mother's side had made that angel when she was a girl. It was moth eaten in places, and mildewed in a few others but it had survived as a symbol. This year, Devon knew that survival meant not just the holiday, but also maybe the hope for a little happiness. It wasn't much to ask for, was it?

She caught herself humming along to one of the carols on the radio in the kitchen, just this morning. With her back to her aunt, she'd been unable to see the small smile on the older woman's face. Maybe this holiday would be easier. Devon certainly hoped so.

Christmas was her very favorite one and she even liked all the corny, old-fashioned traditions that went with it. It wasn't just the tree, which

Uncle Brad promised he would pick out, nor the division of the ornaments into piles so that everyone had their section marked out. She even loved singing the songs, choosing and wrapping all of the gifts. Devon even enjoyed posing for the annual holiday card, though this year she wanted to pass on that. It was too hard to think of who wouldn't be there.

She really wanted to celebrate Christmas though and so she took a deep breath, and opened up the box, pulling things out at random and dumping it all on the floor next to where she sat. The angel was there alright, on the very top of the box and tears sprang immediately to Devon's eyes, making her wipe them away hastily as she stared down at it. Gently, she put it aside and went through the rest of the stuff.

There was the box of handmade ornaments that her great uncle had hand painted. They were as delicate as an eggshell and an even dozen. The fact that they had lasted all these years was amazing to her. She should have figured they would stay intact. Her mother always packed them away very carefully and lovingly and it was why they were still in one piece.

Devon remembered when she and Lucas were little, how these treasured memories used to hang on the top most boughs of the tree, out of their reach but near the front so that they could still be seen. As they grew older, the more delicate ornaments were moved further down the tree and eventually Lucas and Devon were entrusted with hanging them up.

There were so many boxes inside the big crate; each marked so that she knew what was inside. There was a box with her name and one with Lucas' of all the ones that each had made through the school years and even the ones that "Santa" had brought them.

There were the musical ones too; the popping corn, the bus from the Partridge Family, and the various bells that her mother collected. Each one of them was a treasure; each brought the sharp memory of how it had come into their family, and what its emotional value was. She cautiously opened each small box and then put each ornament back, then each box back into the crate, ready to take downstairs.

Devon would always miss her parents and Lucas, especially at Christmas and she knew there would be shed tears. She also knew that there would be space for joy and she wanted that most of all.

Sylvie had forced herself to decorate this year even though her heart was not in it. She was making an effort every bit as much as the rest were. Hadn't she already made plans with Devon to bake some Christmas cookies and maybe go out to look at the neighborhood house decorations?

Thanksgiving had been even harder than Sylvie imagined and she wasn't too sure that this holiday was going to be any easier, not for any of them. She squared her shoulders back and shook her head, getting her mind into it at least. She pulled down the cookie cookbooks and turned the page on the first one, smiling just a little. Really, who could resist a picture of a Santa cookie, complete with a red hat?

By the time Devon made her way downstairs, her aunt had the kitchen table covered with baking supplies and had earmarked more than one page of recipes.

She'd even taken time to turn on the Christmas cd in her player and the room was filled with the sounds of the season.

"Hey, what are we going to make first?" Devon put some effort into her greeting, going so far as to brush a kiss to her aunt's cheek. That part was easy since she loved the woman.

"This one, I think." Sylvie pointed to the image of the chocolate coconut bars.

"It's not exactly Christmassy but you always loved them, remember?"

Devon nodded as she stood next to her aunt, reading the ingredient list over her shoulder.

"It's really easy to make, isn't it?"

"It sure is, and only has a few steps. Come on, you can start by crushing the chocolate wafers for me. Want to use the food processor or the rolling pin?"

Devon didn't even hesitate.

"I want to use the food processor."

"Ok, you start with that and melting the butter. I'll measure out the chocolate chips and the coconut. Oh, and we might as well double the recipe while we're at it. I want to drop off a batch at the local shelter tomorrow."

"That explains the extra boxes of wafers."

The two quickly got to work and with the sound of the holidays surrounding them, soon had two glass pans in the oven. Sylvie poured them each a Pepsi as they waited for the cookies to finish baking.

"What do you want to do next? Drop cookies or cut outs?"

Devon frowned, trying to decide.

"What about that new one, the one with the dried cranberries? That would be easy, don't you think?"

Sylvie nodded, agreeing.

"That sounds like a good plan to me. If we then do the cutouts, we could finish up the day's worth of baking with the cinnamon balls and then we can worry about dinner."

Devon smiled a little.

"Maybe we can call Uncle Brad, ask him to pick up a pizza on his way home. Then, we don't have to worry about cleaning all of this up to make dinner."

Sylvie hugged her niece with a smile of her own.

"I like how you think, Devon. Ok, why don't you give him a call and I'll get out the ingredients for the drop cookies."

She reached for the canisters that held the flour, sugar, and instant milk and set them down on the table, taking time to wash and dry the measuring spoons and cups along with the bowl that had held the wafers and butter.

Once the bars had cooled, they would refrigerate them for two hours before taking them out to cut into squares. It was a good thing that she had the foresight to buy that extra large refrigerator two years ago. That along with the full sized freezer that they kept in the basement made it easy to bake in large quantities. This year with having Devon's help, Sylvie could get to the shelters earlier than usual. It would do them both good to help someone else this year, instead of dwelling on their own misfortunes.

She knew that they'd never be the same. The void would always be there. Sylvie had faith that all of them, especially Devon, would come out on the other side at some point. The girl still had a future to look forward to, and her own family to create and Sylvie wanted that more than anything.

She kept most of those thoughts and worries to herself though. Sylvie had learned long ago that the secret to a good relationship was not to share every errant idea that popped into her head and she found that it seemed to help her with Devon.

"We're getting one large with cheese and pepperoni and one small, loaded," Devon called out cheerfully from the other room.

She had been laughing with her uncle on the phone, which was a rare event in any case. It made Sylvie even more determined to keep everyone busy with hands on work. It was also good that Devon didn't spend a lot of time alone in her room, brooding. She was most often to be found downstairs, offering to help cook or to clean up or even doing her homework at the dining room table, ear buds stuck in her ears.

Chapter Twenty-Nine

Three hours later...

Harrison had just hung up from talking with Aggie. The plan was for him to fly out first thing in the morning to spend a week with her. It had been tricky to rearrange several business matters, but he wanted this relationship to work, long distance or not. He had suggested that Aggie move in with him that would solve everything as far as Harrison could see it.

Aggie was a strong woman, however, who held her ground. The small town in Texas where she had been living was her home. She didn't know if this was going to last between them and she told him that. Aggie also pointed out that she wasn't about to uproot when she didn't have those answers.

He chuckled to himself, enjoying her stubbornness more than he could say as he stripped out of his business suit, carefully hanging it up in his closet. He dumped the rest of his clothes into the laundry bin, giving himself a mental reminder to make sure that his housekeeper took care of it all before his next trip.

Harrison put on his work out clothes, and laced up his shoes, taking the stairs down to the lower level gym where he got to work on some warm up stretches. He frowned a little, having felt what seemed like a twinge between his shoulder blades, but put that down to extra stress at work.

He continued with the stretches, and the twinge went away. He shrugged off the earlier pain, heading over to the bench and getting into position for his presse. Gripping the weight in both hands, he slowly pushed the weight upward, keeping his elbows from locking. Harrison knew that some of the younger guys in gyms were more into power lifting. When they benched, they would drive their feet into the floor in an effort to lift as much weight as possible.

He had no desire to be in competition with any others, much preferring the quiet of his personal gym and letting the young bucks try to outdo each other in public venues.

The pain came suddenly and had him calling out in response. One minute he was finishing his third repetition and the next he felt an unbelievable pain and pressure in his chest. He felt as if someone had picked up one of the dumbbells and thrown it directly at him. Harrison managed to lower the weight back into position, but when he tried to get up, he found himself falling onto his back, and then there was nothing but darkness...

That's where his personal assistant, James, found him not ten minutes later, lying unconscious and unmoving, with his face still in a grimace of pain. James bent down quickly, pressing his finger to Harrison's carotid artery, relieved to find a heartbeat; it was weak but it was still beating. He reached for the cell in his pocket and called 911.

He knew better than to try to move him even as he gave the information, including their exact location in the house. He would wait with Harrison until the paramedics arrived.

....

"Here, let me try."

Mandy took Devon's place in front of the laptop, sitting on the chair in front of her friend's desk.

"You know, it would help if you had some idea of things your brother liked. "

Devon blew the hair out of her eyes, frustration in every movement.

"When Alice told me she was sending this out here, I thought it would be easy to open, but this is insane!"

"She did warn you that the cops had been all over this and none of them could figure out the password that would unlock it." Chloe said helpfully.

Devon just shot her friend a look and then sat down in the chair that Mandy had vacated.

"Yeah, I know but how hard can this be? I mean, he was my brother, not hers. "

"Yeah, I got that. Come on; give me something I can use." Mandy sat, with her hands hovering over the keyboard, waiting patiently as if Devon was holding back.

Chloe reached around and grabbed a notebook and a pen, sitting down on the chair next to Mandy.

"Why don't we try this? We make a list of everything your brother likes and then we try each word and see what works"

It sounded so simple.

Devon looked at Mandy who shrugged her shoulders.

"It can't hurt, Dev. I mean, we've been at this for like hours now."

Once the girls had arrived, they quickly ran upstairs, closing and locking the door behind them, excited about the laptop. They were convinced that it wouldn't take them long at all to unlock the computer, but minutes turned to hours without anything working. Sylvie had left a tray of sandwiches outside the room, promising to do the same for dinner. A quick check of her watch had Chloe realizing that it was almost time for that right now. Time really flew when you were working on solving a computer problem. They had tried everything they could think of but maybe...

Devon took a deep breath.

"Ok, it's better than nothing I guess."

She thought for a few minutes.

They had been close for a brother and sister, but it wasn't like they shared **everything** with each other.

Devon closed her eyes next which had her friends sharing a look. She was trying to imagine Lucas' room before the yellow tape had been put up; trying to remember what he had on his shelves, his walls, even his closet. Lucas was never what Devon would call a neat freak but he took care of his things.

"He liked the Pittsburgh Steelers. He liked the Stones, Green Day, purple, documentaries especially on wars and stuff like that." She slowly opened her eyes to see that Chloe was writing everything down in list form.

"Ok Mandy, try Pittsburgh first. It's kind of a long shot but maybe."

"Nope, that didn't work. Let me try the word "Steelers.""

Mandy typed it in and even played around a while with upper and lower case but shook her head. Nothing seemed to work.

Chloe read each item off her checklist and put an x next to everything that didn't work. It didn't take very long for them to get through the list.

Mandy reached out for Devon, gave her friend's hand a squeeze.

"Maybe we should try again after dinner, you know, take a break, and get away from it for a while."

Devon squeezed back, trying to smile half-heartedly.

"I don't want to go downstairs though; I can't face my aunt and uncle now. I have to figure out the password." Devon sounded both frustrated and determined.

"Sure, sure, I agree with Mandy and we can just eat here. No prob." Chloe tucked the pen behind her left ear and laid the notebook next to the laptop. There was a knock at the door and as she was closest, she opened it to find Dev's aunt there with that tray.

"How's it going girls?"

Sylvie tried not to sound hopeful, but one look at her niece's miserable face told the tale. She focused on bringing in the tray. Sylvie paused to ruffle Devon's hair in a supportive and understanding way before quietly leaving. "Try not to stay up too late, girls," she said as she closed the door behind her.

Dinner was chili and corn bread, Pepsi and chocolate chip cookies. These were all Devon's favorites but she found it hard to swallow.

"Your aunt is great, you know?" Chloe's voice sounded a little muffled as she started eating, spooning up chili and talking with her mouth full as usual.

She had been so hoping that this last connection between her and Lucas would work. Unlocking his computer might tell her why Lucas murdered their parents. If the answers were to be found, it would be on his laptop.

Devon was convinced of that. She called Mandy and Chloe as soon as the laptop arrived. She arranged for a sleepover so that they could work into the night if needed. In the excitement of her plan, Devon never really thought that she wouldn't be able to solve this ongoing mystery.

The girls gave it their best efforts and nothing they tried worked. Mandy and Chloe kept up a steady stream of talk about music and school and other things to give them all that break, even while Mandy watched her friend play with but not really eat much of her food.

"If you don't finish what's in that bowl, then I'm not going to help you anymore tonight, Dev. I mean it. You need to keep up your strength cause who knows what kind of stuff is on this. "

She sounded firm as she tapped the edge of the bowl with her right index finger, holding up a handful of the cookies with the other hand, and waving them back and forth.

"Come on; eat up like a good girl and I'll let you have your cookies."

It got a laugh out of Devon as she spooned up the rest of her chili and made the other two girls smile together.

"My mother used that on me when I was little, bugged me big time but it works so..., eat your cookies now and we'll try another angle."

"Listen to her," Chloe laughed, nudging Mandy. "Talks like she works for the CIA or something."

"You never know, maybe I'll be recruited for my top notch computer skills."

Devon laughed a little at that one.

"I'm more than willing to let you have the credit for breaking the password. After all, with my family rep, I'd never get that kind of job."

Chapter Thirty

The phone started ringing as soon as her hands were in the soapy water so Sylvie called out for Brad to answer it. While she finished the dishes, she waited to find out who could be calling. She was only half-interested. Knowing her husband, it was most likely something to do with work.

Brad practically lived and breathed work and she had been amazed to see him put that aside long enough to be fully attending at his brother's funeral. Alright, maybe he patted the pocket holding his phone at the end of the mass. However, on the plus side, he never once reached for it and Sylvie would have known, standing right next to him in church.

Her thoughts idly drifted upstairs to where the three girls were, pleased that Devon had made such nice friends. Sylvie had been so worried that Devon would feel like an outsider but she was such an outgoing girl and doing well since the move. Sylvie was so lost in her thoughts that it took Brad several minutes of saying her name, the last time rather harshly, before she responded.

"Sorry about that. Who was on the phone?"

There was silence from her husband, which wasn't usual.
Sylvie turned from the sink and took in the stricken look on his face, grabbing a dishtowel and drying her hands.

"What is it?"

"That was James on the phone. It looks like my father had a heart attack."

"That can't be true. He's the healthiest man of his years that I've ever met. Is James sure?"

Brad blinked a few times, and then nodded.

"He found him unconscious on the floor in his home gym and had him rushed to the emergency room. The paramedics treated him at the house for what they believed to be a heart attack."

"He's sending the private plane." Brad said as an afterthought, leaving the kitchen to head upstairs to pack.

"Who's sending the plane?" Sylvie was confused. Didn't he just say that his father.... Oh, right. James. She had forgotten about her father-in-law's personal assistant. It was a good thing that James had been present when the attack happened; they could all be thankful for his presence.

"I'll be right up, I have to call Mandy's mother, see if she can take Devon for a few days."

Not again, was all that she was thinking even as she reached for the phone. She found what she wanted in the small book she had and then she punched in the number. Brad had been so devastated by the murders. If Harrison died now after all that happened? Sylvie didn't know how any of them would manage to go on.

She fought back the fear that was threatening to swallow her whole and managed to sound cheerful when she heard Mandy's mother pick up the phone.

"Phoebe, this is Sylvie. Oh, no worries, the girls are having a great time. I need to ask you a big favor."

Phoebe was the calmest, most capable woman that Sylvie knew. They had never been very friendly in the past with one another because they just didn't seem to have much in common. That changed a little once Devon had moved in; there were a few times that Sylvie and Phoebe had shared coffee and a few lunches.

With Brad upstairs doing the bulk of the packing, she filled her neighbor in on what had happened and Phoebe readily agreed to help.

"Of course, Sylvie, we'd love to have her and you don't have to worry while you're gone. Take as long as you need."

This from a woman who ran a catering service from her home, volunteered for the high school PTA and other organizations, along with raising four children and managing a busy husband and house.

Assured though that this was the best decision, she thanked her, hung up, and went upstairs to fill Devon in on the change in plans.

....

Devon picked up her bear, hugging him for a little moral support. If either of the other two girls thought it was childish, they never acted that way. It wasn't like she slept with Aloysius; it just made her feel good having him there with her. The bear usually sat on the chair in Devon's room where she could see him while she did her homework. If she talked to him occasionally, that was her business. Mandy and Chloe didn't have to know that, and Devon wasn't going to share that news with either girl. That would not be cool. Devon had learned how to fit in, what to say and what not to say, though she knew deep down that she could probably have told them anything, including the stuff with the bear.

She still didn't want to chance it and then...... Devon looked down at him, and then back to Mandy who was trying variations of ideas and still hitting zero for her efforts.

"Aloysius"

"Huh?" Mandy and Chloe both turned around in their chairs, looking at her.

"A-l-o-y-s-i-u-s" Devon spelled it out slowly.

"Go ahead, give that one a try and use the A in uppercase."

234

The bear? You could almost see it in their expressions as Mandy and Chloe just stared at Devon. Mandy shrugged, and turned back to the laptop, carefully typing out the name the way that Dev had spelled it. The laptop blinked twice and then it unlocked.

The girls all stared at it, biting back screams as they half screamed, half whispered

"OMG!"

"I have to tell you Dev, that I thought you were going nuts there, but look!" Mandy stared at the computer again, still feeling a little crazed with victory.

Devon watched the home screen as it came to life, with Lucas' icons scattered around.

Mandy got out of her chair and nudged her friend to sit down.

"You should be the one to go through his stuff. I'd start by going through his documents first."

Devon sat down and opened up the "My Documents."

There were a lot of them in here, well over a hundred. She slowly scanned down them, hoping that a name would pop out at her, and it would be the right one.

Devon didn't want to have to go through each and every one, but she'd do it if it seemed like nothing else was going to do the trick.

There was an actual file with her name in it and it was dated two months before the killings. She double clicked and up it came in the form of a letter and it was addressed to her.

"Devon,

I don't know if I'm ever going to send this to you or not but I had to write this stuff down.

Now that I'm staring at a blank screen, it doesn't seem as easy to do that but here goes.

I overheard something that you need to know and I don't know how else to say it but straight out.

....

Five seconds later... Talk about timing!

At that very moment, there was a knock at the door! Devon quickly closed down the document and the laptop, so that when Aunt Sylvie opened the door, she just saw three girls sitting at the desk. Sylvie was too preoccupied by the phone call that they had just received to notice that anything was amiss.

"Girls, I really hate to break things up." She turned her attention to Devon. "Your grandfather had a heart attack, Devon."

236

"What? Grandpa? But he's like super healthy." She sounded confused.

"I know how it sounds. He did have a heart attack though and we're going to have to rush to the airport." Sylvie held up her hand as her niece jumped out of her chair and headed for her closet.

"Not you, Devon. I talked to Mandy's mother and she agreed to put you up for a few days. We just couldn't drag you with us after everything that happened, and we can't exactly take you out of school for this either."

Both Chloe and Mandy got up to stand with their friend.

"It's Ok, Mrs. Fielding. We'll help her pack up her stuff and meet you downstairs." Mandy, as always, took charge.

With a soft sigh of relief, Sylvie nodded and then hugged her daughter and the other two girls before stepping back.

"Thank you. You have no idea what a relief that is. Your parents are on their way over so if you could hurry this up? My husband is already packing and I'm doing the same but I'd like us to all leave together."

Once Sylvie left, Chloe sat back down on the bed while Mandy and Devon packed.

"So damn close too." She looked over at Mandy and then back at Devon.

"You want to boot it back up, read the rest of the letter?"

Chloe was trying hard to contain her excitement ever since they had broken into the brother's laptop and found the document. This could be the answer to the big, dark secret hanging over her friend's head but she knew it wasn't really up to her.

Sure enough, Devon was shaking her head as she put the laptop back in its case. Carefully, she placed it on the top shelf of her closet, shutting the door firmly.

"Look, my grandfather's in the hospital with a heart attack, in Chicago. I can't think about anything else right now, Ok? Let's just get me packed and over to Mandy's. At least I know how to open the laptop. I can wait a while longer."

"Yeah, sure, Dev, no problem."

Mandy was nodding her head, agreeing with what her friend had said even though she was just as disappointed as Chloe. However, they had to take care of Devon first. The laptop wasn't going anywhere and they had plenty of time to get back to it.

Together, they spent the next few minutes getting Devon ready so that they were downstairs as Mandy's mother pulled up in front.

Devon gave her aunt and uncle a quick hug, reminding them to give her very best to her grandfather. She slipped into the backseat with Mandy and Chloe while her aunt and uncle got into the cab that had pulled up in the driveway.

Chapter Thirty-One

"Mr. James Richards?"

"Yes?" He got out of his seat as a man wearing blue scrubs with a stethoscope around his neck, approached.

"I'm Dr. Meuit and I am in charge of Mr. Fielding's care while he's here. Let's step this way and I'll try to fill you in." The man was about five ten and had strong, muscular arms. He spoke with a slight accent but James couldn't quite place it.

Dr. Meuit led James down the hall to a small room and took a seat. Once James had been seated, he continued.

"Mr. Fielding did not have the usual form of a heart attack."

"He didn't?" James was puzzled because it sure looked that way when he found his boss lying on the floor.

Dr. Meuit shook his head.

"I'm sure that's how it looked and the paramedics called it in as a heart attack, but once we did preliminary tests, we found that wasn't the case at all. What Mr. Fielding suffered is what is known as a spasm of the coronary artery." He pointed to a series of pictures to emphasize his point. "This means that when these arteries spasm on and off, they reduce the blood supply to the heart."

James studied the images. They helped even though he wasn't all that well versed on medical issues. "So, how is he?"

The doctor turned around in his chair to face James as he continued to discuss his patient's situation.

"He's very fortunate that the amount of damage done was minimal. The attack must have happened within minutes of your finding him and getting him the proper treatment. That allows me to say that he should have a very good outcome.

In checking his records that were sent over by his primary physician, I found that he was being treated for high cholesterol. He was only at the very lowest level for that to be of any true concern, however. Except for that particular medication, Mr. Fielding appeared to have been in excellent health.

He's conscious but I do not advise visitors just yet as we have more tests to conduct." The doctor paused for a minute before continuing.

"According to my brief conversation with him, it appears that his particular set of spasms was most likely caused by extreme emotional stress. Now I heard the news reports several months back about the murders." The doctor watched James' expression when he spoke about this past event. "This could be a delayed reaction coupled by the fact that he flat out works too hard in a very demanding profession.

I seriously doubt that he is going to remain spasm free unless he manages his work activities a little better. He needs to learn how to delegate." It was standard advice that Dr. Meuit gave to most of the patients he had. Very few actually tried to make any effort in changing the hectic lifestyles that had brought them to the hospital in the first place.

"For now, we'll keep him comfortable once the tests come back. We will most likely be putting him on medications such as a calcium challenge blocker. That's to reduce the muscle tightness in his chest." The doctor got to his feet and checked his watch. He had a surgery that he had to perform. "I'll keep you posted, but if you want to contact his surviving son, now might be a good time. He's too healthy overall to have these problems and considering the high stress he's experiencing, I don't want to take any chances."

James nodded, trying hard to write everything down so that he could explain it to Brad when he got there. This doctor was thorough, but very business like, as he simply presented his case.

"I contacted his son from the ambulance. He and his wife will be here by tomorrow at the latest."

"That's good. Now, I need to get to the operating room for another surgery. I'll be back later to let you know the rest of my treatment plan."

With that said, Dr. Meuit headed back down the hall.

James went off in search of an area where he could use his cell. This section of the hospital had a dead zone where he couldn't get a signal. He needed to contact Ruth to let her know what to expect so that she could handle things at her end until Harrison was considered fit to leave the hospital.

As he was hanging up and heading back to the waiting area, James wondered if it were even possible for his employer to make what would be enormous changes in his life and work style.

Nevertheless, maybe, just maybe, this was the wakeup call that Harrison needed. He and Ruth talked about it a lot, how the man was always working, or thinking about work, even when he wasn't actually at the office.

The only time in his memory when that changed was during the trip to Erie to handle the funeral and other details surrounding the murders and suicide. It wasn't exactly a vacation, but Harrison rarely took those.

During that week away, James heard from Harrison only twice and Ruth, not at all, which was very unlike him. It did prove however, that Harrison could put work aside when needed.

He'd just have to have a very good incentive. Being the head of the still grieving family might be what it would take to convince him that he would have to change.
Of course, he was also spending more time traveling back and forth to Texas to visit Aggie. However, those trips didn't slow him down as far as his work schedule went.

....
It was yet another airport with another trip and still in the same year. The difference this time, Brad thought as he settled in the seat behind the pilot, was that they were in a private plane so he could stretch out, and even sleep if he chose to.

There was a bed in the back, along with a full bathroom and a larger than usual galley with a flight attendant, who was making coffee and a light snack to tide them over until their next meal.

Brad rarely thought about the luxuries that were such a part of his father's life, but even he was aware that very few people could call up a plane of their own to take them back and forth across the country at a minute's notice.

Even going through the airport security had been made easier by the mere mention of the Fielding plane. They were ready for takeoff almost as soon as both passengers were belted into their seats, minutes after presenting their

ID's at the ticket counter. Leaving in the early evening made their progress that much faster. There weren't any other scheduled flights so the airport was practically deserted, leaving only a handful of staff.

Brad appreciated not having to wait, almost willing the pilot to get them there as quickly as possible. It had been hard enough to arrive in Erie to find that not only had Greg and Susannah been gone, but so had Lucas.

At the time, he had mentally cursed the slowness of the airlines with the two changes in planes that had taken forever to get them back home.

It was a good thing that he and Sylvie only had to fly to Chicago this time around. The traveling wouldn't be as long and they wouldn't be so exhausted.

Chapter Thirty-Two

There was a faint light in the room when Harrison opened his eyes and saw the figure dozing in a chair next to his bed.

"Aggie." His voice was scratchy and low but her eyes instantly snapped open, her hand automatically reaching out for his.

"Harrison Fielding, this is not the kind of call a woman like me expects to receive late at night." Her voice was stern, like that of a prim schoolteacher and he smiled briefly.

"James has a nice telephone voice, or so people tell me." His was almost teasing as she tugged her hand away.

Aggie's voice, when she spoke again, held that of tears forced back.

"You scared me half to death, Harrison. I dropped the phone and almost broke it when I tried to hang up. If Brenda hadn't been visiting, it would still be lying on the floor with the receiver off the hook."

"I'm glad your daughter was with you. Did she drive you to the airport?"

"Yes she did and I caught the next flight out."

"That's good, and I'm glad I'm still alive, even if it means that I get chewed out for frightening you." His eyes met hers. It couldn't have been easy for her.

Harrison would never suggest that a plane be sent for her. However, he had been unconscious when James had called. It was good that his assistant had also been aware of Aggie's preferences in travel.

The private plane was fine if they were together. Aggie didn't like how it looked to go to the airport and find a plane waiting just for her. She complained that it was a giant waste of perfectly good money, which was right of course. The difference was that Harrison didn't mind paying for such conveniences while Aggie clearly did.

It was yet another fascinating aspect of this woman and he felt very warm all over, waking to find her beside him.

"Have the doctors spoken to you or James yet?"

"No, they haven't talked to me. I think they're waiting for Brad to get here which won't be until early tomorrow."

That part had irked her; the fact that as his girlfriend, Aggie wasn't considered to be entitled to much more information than the fact that Harrison was resting comfortably. She could see that for herself but the rest of the details would only be given to next of kin. James knew more due to his having a limited power of attorney, but he didn't tell her anything either.

"James would be glad to tell you what they said. You just have to ask."

Aggie smiled, even though Harrison still couldn't see it for himself that James resented her. He resented the strength of the growing relationship, and would only speak to Aggie when it was necessary, but she wasn't about to bring all that up to Harrison. If he couldn't see this for himself, she would be the last one to bring it to his attention.

Aggie knew that her lover had had numerous prior relationships, but this one was different. Harrison was not just spending all his free time with her, he was sharing himself. Harrison shared his personal details, even discussed some of his many business dealings. Both of those things meant more to her than the near constant spoiling of her that he did whenever they were together.

To put it plainly, Harrison was becoming as devoted to Aggie as she was to him. When the call came, she had never considered not flying out to him.

It seemed to surprise, maybe even shock James a little when Aggie announced that she would be on the next plane out. But what did he expect? This was the man she loved, not just some casual acquaintance. Of course, she would be there and she knew that Brad wouldn't object. If anything, he would wonder where Aggie was, unless it was right here by his father's side, where she belonged.

Harrison watched the flow of emotions over his lover's face as he lay there. A minute or two later a nurse came bustling inside to check his vitals and then she informed Aggie that visiting hours were long past and that she needed to leave. Her patient required quiet and rest. She practically shooed Aggie along, all brisk efficiency and a no nonsense attitude. No other approach would work with Aggie. She assured Harrison that she had a place to sleep and then out she went, without telling him that she meant a hotel room. It would be too much to show up at the house, even though she had a key and the security code.

Aggie couldn't simply go there and establish herself as a pseudo mistress of the place, even if that's what they both thought her to be. No, it was better that she stayed tucked out of sight for a while. The hotel was a short distance from the hospital and she would be back early.

Besides, she was already spent not just from the travel, but also from the overwhelming fear that she would arrive too late, and would find him already gone. It was a fear Aggie lived with constantly, having survived three husbands. She knew Harrison to be a complete health nut, but that didn't stop the fear.

Maybe she just wasn't destined to outlive a man. This was despite the fact that she privately considered fries and chocolate ice cream to be part of the food pyramid.

Aggie didn't hide much from Harrison except for her food choices. She always made sure to clear out her freezer of her favorite Hagen Daz before he came for a visit. She spent the rest of his visit trying desperately to fight her cravings for fries instead of a baked potato when they went out to eat. Aggie smiled a little to herself though; he probably already knew that about her anyway.

Even though she had wanted to stay at the hospital, she was still grateful to fall into the soft bed in her room. Her shoes were still on her feet, but she could already feel the tension start to ebb from her body.

The nurse was right of course; she needed rest if she was going to face Harrison tomorrow and help him with whatever the doctor had decided would be major changes in his lifestyle. Aggie understood that much, even if most of her information came from the net. All she knew was that he had a heart attack. Aggie was determined that tomorrow she would learn the rest. She was grateful that James had found Harrison so quickly, even if she didn't like the man personally.

After a few minutes, she got up and set the alarm clock for the next day. Checking the small booklet of services available, she found out what time she would need to call room service for breakfast the next day. Aggie made a mental note to do that as soon as she got up, so that she could shower, change, and be ready when the food arrived.

She could be efficient too, a skill she had learned while on the job, back in the day when she had first started working for Harrison.

Chapter Thirty-Three

7 months later...

Devon had wanted to finish reading the letter from her brother, but life somehow managed to keep intruding with all sorts of demands. If she were being truthful with herself, she would admit that she was putting off reading the letter. Somehow, without her friends in the room with her, it all got scary again. Devon wasn't all that certain now that she wanted to know what Lucas had to say. Maybe someday but not right now, she told herself.

Schoolwork was a major distraction and for a young girl who still had plans of attending college in less than two years, that meant a few trips to schools that were what her Aunt Sylvie called "possibilities."

When she first talked about her college plans, Devon had discussed attending Smith, which was fine with everyone. However, the last few months had seen a change from Smith to that of Boston University where she could study journalism.

It was a decision that worried her aunt and uncle. They thought that perhaps she had made this choice as a way to hold onto the memory of her brother. Both MIT and BU as it was affectionately known were located in the same city. Devon knew that no matter what she said, she'd never convince them otherwise so she didn't even try.

She knew what she wanted; the money was there in her college fund. After all, she'd be a legal adult by that first day in her new dorm, so there wasn't much else to be said. What was more annoying was that her friends Chloe and Mandy also expressed some concerns.

"Geez, Dev, that's like half a world away isn't it? I mean, you'd have to find all new friends again." Mandy had a point though. Devon would have to start all over again. If there was one thing that she had learned so far, it was that she could do more than just survive. She could have a life.

Mandy had been tapping her pen against her braces, which she did every time she tried to make an important point.

Chloe was blunter in expressing herself.

"You can't live your life for your brother, you know. There are lots of great schools around here that can teach you journalism."

"Yeah, I know. I could go to Kansas, Iowa, Arizona, even Indiana." Devon ticked off each one on the fingers of her right hand.

"It's a fact that BU is the number Two University for journalism in the entire country. The entire country, guys." She shrugged her shoulders as she sat curled up on her desk chair.

"That's big, and it's the reason I'm going there, not because it would put me close to where Lucas would have been." Devon paused to twist a strand of hair into a curl and then released it. It was hard enough to explain all of this to her aunt and uncle, and now she had to try to make her friends see why she had made this decision.

"I know he's gone, that he's never coming back, and that I have to live my life for myself and not anyone else. This is for me and I'll be just fine on my own there. It's not like they don't have counselors and stuff and the dorm situation is pretty safe. I can have the same place for the entire four years. They even help in roommate selection or I can have my own room which is personally what I want."

Both girls had been silent while Devon talked. Everything that she had said made sense. You couldn't plan your future based on what other people wanted for you, but then Mandy spoke up from where she was sitting on the large floor rug.

"Ever think about the fact that we're going to miss you? I'm sticking to the local University of Montana to study computer science. You know my parents have no money to send me further away. I'll be one of those commuters that you hear about and I'll be fine." She paused and reached out to tug at her friend's pink slippered foot playfully.

"You can study journalism there, Dev."

Chloe shrugged and stretched on Devon's bed.

"I'm not spending another four years of my life in cold weather, shoveling my way out of my own house and having to wear layers of clothing. That's why I'm heading off to beautiful California. The weather's hot all the time, I can even go surfing on my vacations, and I'm going to study at Berkeley.

I've decided to become an electrical engineer. I like taking things apart to find out how they work and how to make them better and this is a perfect fit for me." She smiled winningly over at her friend.

"They don't have journalism as an undergrad major, but they do have it as a grad program. Maybe you could study something else and come with me. Be somewhere warm for once."

Devon just laughed and shook her head.

"We're all going our own way, forging our own paths as my uncle calls it." She sighed a little because she was really going to miss them both. The three girls had become close, closer she realized than she'd been with any of her so called former friends back in Erie. It didn't even hurt anymore to be shut out of that past life of hers.

Devon had made a new one and according to her aunt, what she was experiencing now, this scared feeling of going out on her own, was perfectly normal. That's what she liked best, feeling normal again.

She promised herself that she would get to Lucas' letter one of these days. Right now, she had a life to live, as she looked around her room at the boxes still stacked there, cluttering up her things. This might be the best time to start going through some of them.

"Hey guys, why don't we change the subject and you can help me sort out my mom's stuff."

Chloe and Mandy exchanged a look. This was a new and big step for their friend but they both got to their feet.

"It works for me." Chloe, still a woman of few words most of the time, headed over to where the stack was, and turned back to Devon.

"Want to just start in order?"

Devon took a breath and nodded, going over to clear some room on her bed.

"Why don't we open the box there and just dump it all on the bed?"

"You should make piles, Dev. You know the have to keep, and the have to toss." That was Mandy for you, ever practical and to the point, which Devon always admired.

"What about the undecided pile?" Chloe thought that just having two might be too hard.

How do you decide on some of this stuff anyway?

However, Mandy was already shaking her head.

"My mom told me once that you only need two piles when you're cleaning out your room. The stuff you keep and the stuff you toss. Anything else is a waste. Come on, we'll help you, Dev."

It didn't take that long to get everything sorted out; not when Devon had two willing and very economical friends to help her go through it all. Of course, it was easier for Mandy and Chloe since it wasn't their stuff, but in the end, there were only two piles left.

A very small pile easily fit into one small crate that was taped up and shoved into the back of Devon's closet. What was left was stuffed into six large garbage bags that were dragged downstairs and left by the front door before being hauled into her aunt's black SUV trunk. The girls left shortly afterwards, with promises to call Devon in a day or two.

Tomorrow, Devon would help her Aunt Sylvie in unloading it all at the local thrift store downtown.

As she made the last trip upstairs to make sure she didn't miss anything that might have fallen out of one of the bags, she looked around her room.

Devon knew that she had come a long way, and it was almost the anniversary of her parent's murders and her brother's subsequent suicide. Once her application to BU had been mailed and then accepted, she'd be on her way east while her friends would go on their own journeys.

They promised to keep in touch via Facebook and Twitter, but Devon knew that promises like these were easily broken once they all were settled.

A smile came over her face as she saw the sun peeking out from behind the clouds that had covered the sky for most of the earlier part of the day.

As Devon got ready to leave her room, she paused, her hand on the doorknob. She'd been putting this off for too long now and really, what was the point? Wasn't this what she wanted? Devon needed to know why Lucas had killed their parents. If he had taken the time to leave her a message, then she needed to take time right now and find out the answers. With a determined turn of her body, she walked over to the closet and reaching high on her toes, grabbed his laptop. Sitting down on her bed with the computer on her lap, she quickly typed in his password and waited. Once it had unlocked, she double clicked on "documents." Finding her file name, she double clicked it open and sat down to read....

To be continued...

Funny how being dead changes everything. My grandfather is recovering from heart troubles, my sister is planning on what college to go to, and I'm kind of selfish here but I'm glad she picked BU. It's a great school and yeah, she gets that it's near where I was going to go, but that's not why she picked it.

My sister is a great writer; she's got that column at the local high school paper. Did you know that? Yeah, writing about local events, the social stuff, but it means she gets to sorta hang with the popular crowd even if it's just for interviews and stuff. She's really good too and such a fast typist so journalism is a good fit for her.

And she's so ready for this. I never thought I'd be the one to say it, you know, being dead and all but she's ready. She'll take the extra year to work on keeping her GPA up and when she graduates and moves on, she'll be ready.

I kinda wish she didn't read the rest of my letter to her though. Not yet anyway. I still have that secret to tell her and so far all she knows is that there's a secret.

Me and my dragging it all out. I should have just told her, straight out, the minute I found out instead of putting it in a document on my computer and then what? Hoping she'd figure out the password all on her own? That was a long shot alright and I'm more than shocked that she figured it out, though I did give her a clue back there in that conference room.

How was I to know that she'd ever need to find my note? I only know part of the secret. What I know changed everything and it's still not the entire secret. Wonder if Devon will ever learn the rest of it.....

Acknowledgements

It may take a village to raise a child, but it takes almost as many people to write a book. So many great and supportive people helped me achieve my dream of becoming an author.

Thanks to Dr. Jason Cardinali for providing the detailed exercise routines, and for reading excerpts of my work. Most of all, thanks for listening to me talk about my book and characters.

Thanks to my husband, who helped with his own editing, and making suggestions on how to improve on what he read. Thanks also for being supportive of my many writing meetings.

Thanks to Camille, my "fearless leader" and local liaison for NANOWRIMO. Your helpful advice on how to make my novel the best it can be was very much appreciated. Thanks too for enjoying it almost as much as I do and for being a great cheering squad, especially when I didn't think I could finish.

Thanks to my sister-in-law, Shawn, for continuing to be excited and supportive of my writing efforts.

Thanks to Owen for encouraging me to follow my dreams.

Thanks to Bernice and Ron who kept asking if I was still writing. I think they want to read this as much as anyone else on my list.

Thanks to William R. Vitanyi, Jr., for starting the first Build-A-Book project and sparking a renewed interest in writing.

Thanks to the members of the Chapter One Writer's Group in Waukesha, Wisconsin. Thanks to Norm Bruce from that group for suggesting that his writer's group become involved with their own Build-A-Book project. It's how I first met all of you wonderfully talented people, even if it was all online.

I hope you all enjoy the finished book as much as I do.

About the author:

KB Manz enjoys photography; the cover image is her own. When she's not creating characters and situations, she spends time reading, scrap booking, photography, walking and doing embroidery.

In the summer of 2009, along with thirty-three other people, she co-wrote *"Lara's Gems"* for the first Build-A-Book project.

Her second co-written novel was also a Build-A-Book project. The book was called *"Where Do I Begin: One Woman's Story."* This second venture was written along with members of the Chapter One Writers' Group, located in Waukesha, Wisconsin. It was an entirely online project.

In November of 2014, through Blurb.com, she participated in NANOWRIMO; aka National Novel Writing Month. "Can't take back yesterday" was written as part of this thirty day, fifty thousand word minimum writing project and is her first solo work. KB lives in Northwestern Pennsylvania with her family and is already hard at work on her next novel. This second book promises to reveal the secret!